WHO IS
THE NEXT?

WHO IS
THE NEXT?

Henry Kitchell Webster

PERENNIAL LIBRARY
Harper & Row, Publishers
New York, Cambridge, Hagerstown, Philadelphia, San Francisco
London, Mexico City, São Paulo, Sydney

First PERENNIAL LIBRARY edition published 1981.

ISBN: 0-06-080539-0

81 82 83 84 10 9 8 7 6 5 4 3 2 1

CONTENTS

Who Is the Next?

THE LINDSTROM PLACE

THE law offices of Prentiss, Ford, Scheidenham and Murray had pretty well succumbed to the somnolent influences of a warm late July afternoon; most of the partners who weren't away on their vacations were out playing golf, probably, or taking after-luncheon naps at their clubs. There was nothing but the bare bones of routine to keep any one awake, and hardly enough of that. When Prentiss Murray came in about four o'clock, Miss Foster smiled him a somewhat more than secretarial welcome. She was really glad to see him. Probably when he'd looked over and signed the letters on his desk he'd tell her she might as well go home. But if he didn't, there'd at least be something to do.

She had a message for him so she followed him into his private office. But he spoke first.

"You haven't heard anything more from the mad woman, have you? She hasn't been trying to date me up to fly with her this afternoon?"

Miss Foster knew whom he meant, of course: it was

his young ward, Camilla Lindstrom. Camilla had bought an airplane and it was to have been delivered to-day. She'd been learning to fly and had got her private pilot's license only about a week ago.

The boss was always groaning and growling about his guardianship of this young woman as one of the principal thorns of his existence and pretended to consider her a pest. But he was nuts about her, really. Weren't men the limit! Here was one of the smartest lawyers in town, a bachelor of forty, who ought to know his way about if anybody did, and yet this nineteen-year-old kid could talk him into practically anything, even into an advance of a whole quarter's allowance to buy an airplane with, which he made no bones of admitting he was scared to death of.

No gleam of these reflections, however, appeared either in Miss Foster's face or in her voice as she said, "No, there's been no word from her. They telephoned from Oak Ridge, though. Old Mr. Lindstrom wants you to come out for dinner with him to-night—'If you possibly could,' his secretary said. It's something serious, or she seems to think it is. She said six-thirty, but that means seven-thirty, because they don't keep daylight saving time."

Evidently Murray thought it was serious too, for all

he said, after sitting perfectly still for about ten seconds, was "I'll talk to her." Over annoyances that he regarded as trivial he swore a great deal and made a terrible fuss, generally; but when he saw real trouble ahead he was as quiet as the statue of a man playing poker. She picked up the telephone on his desk and put the call through, and when it was completed she handed the instrument over to him and would have gone out if he had not detained her with a nod toward the telephone on the other desk. She knew what that meant, so she sat down to it with her notebook and pencil and wrote out the whole conversation in shorthand.

There was nothing to it. After he'd told old Lindstrom's secretary that he'd come to dinner he stalled along politely in order to give her a chance to spill anything that was on her mind, but apparently there was nothing she wanted to spill. Parsons, her name was, and Miss Foster didn't like her voice.

"Well, we drew blank that time," he remarked, with a rueful grin, to Miss Foster as they both hung up. "There's something ugly going on out there, though. I'd like to know what that young lady has up her sleeve. Have you any observations to make?"

"I've never seen her, of course," Miss Foster observed. "What does she look like?"

"She's a French blonde, if you know what I mean. Her skin doesn't match her hair. In her thirties, I should say, though she may be younger."

"Don't you think it's the usual thing?" Miss Foster said. "Men as old as Mr. Lindstrom are supposed to be pretty easy to marry."

"That's Camilla's idea," Murray said. "Maybe that's all there is to it. But her voice didn't sound quite like that to me. There was an edge on it but not just the kind of edge there'd have been if she'd known I was going to be asked to draw a settlement to-night, or a new codicil to the will. She may have found out about Camilla's flying, but it didn't sound like that, either. More fright than triumph, somehow."

This was one of the things Miss Foster never could get used to. What right, she asked herself, had a middle-aged golf and bridge playing corporation lawyer to perceptions or intuitions as fine as that? He was probably right, too; generally was. But, as before, there was nothing in her face to betray these reflections. She offered no comment on his guess; just sat still and let him think.

After a minute of it he signed his letters and told her she might as well run along home. There wouldn't be anything more to-night.

He waited until after she had gone, though, to go out and tell the girl on the telephone switchboard to leave his phone plugged in on the main line when she left. He called up his apartment and told his man that if any one wanted him he could be found at the office until seven, and then settled down to read galley proof on a brief, satisfied that if Camilla did want him for anything she could get through to him without delay. The damned kid made him more trouble than all the rest of his clients put together!

This time, though, she didn't bother him—at all events, she didn't telephone. She might have given him a ring, he thought, just to tell him that she was safely down after her first flight in her new ship. She was all right, of course. She'd have taken one of the pilots with her on her first hop.

At seven o'clock he got his car, a convertible coupé, out of the down-town garage in the next block and started for Oak Ridge, the queer anomalous suburb out on the northwest side where old Oscar Lindstrom had lived for nearly sixty years.

Lindstrom's fortune, the whole of his long successful career, interested Prentiss Murray, since it seemed to him to be the outcome of just one wise, or lucky, decision. He'd come from Norway with his young wife and a comfortable little Norwegian fortune of twenty thousand dollars or so, to Chicago, intending to settle there and grow up with the town. They arrived on an October evening in 1871 while the town was in the actual process of burning to the ground. And Lindstrom's great decision was not to go on and settle somewhere else, but to wait for the embers to cool and seize the opportunity that was open to a man with some really free ready money.

It was the only audacious thing he ever did. From then on he was always on the safe side, steadily, but not too fast, getting richer, until now, at eighty-five, his fortune was more than five, and might amount to ten, million dollars. He hadn't been infallibly sagacious, by any means, even in his investments. His guess about Oak Ridge, for instance, had been conspicuously wrong. But by sticking to platitudes, solemnly pronounced in a slightly foreign accent which he'd never got rid of, he'd managed to have attributed to him a profound wisdom that was almost legendary. In the same way, without ever having done, as far as Murray could make out, a single act of large generosity, just by giving methodically to the more conventional religious and charitable organizations, he was reputed to be a public spirited philanthropist.

He and his wife had alighted at Oak Ridge in the first instance simply because it wasn't burning up and was well to leeward of the fire. But they'd stayed there because it had been Lindstrom's idea that this village was destined to be the city's great residential suburb. When he began getting rich he bought a piece of about twenty acres in the outskirts of the town, running back to the river, and upon this he built his red-brick mansard-roofed mansion, with an ornate cupola on the top which could be seen for miles and was much admired at the time. But Chicago discovered the lake just about then and began rolling out north and south along the shores of it, and Oak Ridge for years never grew at all. It continued to be served by its three trains a day to and from town, and the rich black fields on either side of the Lindstrom place were devoted to garden truck, mostly onions. About the only traffic on the old Telegraph Pike, which ran past their front gate, was a procession of creaking farmers' wagons from midnight to three in the morning carrying their produce into the Haymarket. Lindstrom, however, stuck it out, built a high brick wall around the place, except on the side where the river bounded it, and let his wife devote herself to flower gardens. It was about the only pleasure she ever had, poor thing.

She was a nervous invalid, her condition ranging from a gentle melancholy hypochondria to spells of manic excitement during which she had to be seriously looked after. She never could bear meeting strangers and practically never left the place. They had one child, a boy, whom they named Charles, born in 'seventy-five, but this exhausted her capacity for child-bearing.

When the boy was fifteen the old man sent him abroad to complete his education, and for the next ten years he lived there, in Germany and Switzerland mostly, growing up into a pleasant, rather ineffectual young man with a great deal of charm; harmless, you'd have said, in any conceivable event. And in making that prediction you'd have been utterly and tragically wrong.

Somewhere abroad he met Camilla Fairweather of Philadelphia, fell in love with her, and at twenty-five came home and married her without previously obtaining his father's consent. Until the ghastly ending of his responsible life this was his only act of rebellion. Camilla was due to inherit a comfortable fortune some day, but until that should happen, she was dependent upon her husband, and he in turn was under the thumb of that implacable old image, his father. He summoned the pair home to live with him and his invalid wife in the mansion at Oak Ridge; Charles obeyed, and there they lived for twenty years.

Old Lindstrom, under the pretense of inducting his son into his affairs, made a messenger boy of him and paid him the salary of a competent clerk. The unfortunate pair had two children, a boy whom they named Eric, born in 1901, and ten years later a girl, Camilla. Ten years later again there came what looked like a rift in the clouds, for Charles's wife inherited the Fairweather fortune, which had been impending so long, of close to a million dollars.

It was only a few months later that Charles went suddenly mad and killed his wife with a razor with which he had been in the act of shaving. He made an attempt, unhappily not successful, to take his own life with the same instrument. The doctors, in accordance with the highest ethics of their profession, succeeded in keeping him alive, and he was locked up in a private asylum for the violently insane, where he had lived, if you could call it that, until his death a few years later.

The belated fortune, though, which had fallen in too late to do the murdered woman much good, did effect the release of the children. Under her will it was divided between them. Eric, coming into his share on the attainment of his majority, went abroad to study art. The will had appointed two guardians for Camilla: one of them her father, and the other Prentiss Murray, of the firm that had been doing old man Lindstrom's law business for him for the last half-century.

There was nothing perfunctory about the way in which Murray took on his duties. To him old Lindstrom's idea that the stricken bewildered child should go on living in that tragic household with him and her grandmother, more nearly mad than ever after the tragedy, a governess and the servants, was simply unthinkable. He spent weeks finding a school for her, and when his plans were all laid bullied Lindstrom into agreeing to them.

Murray had developed a technique for dealing with the old gentleman which, sparingly used, always produced desirable results. He would tell the old man what he really thought of him in the most outrageous terms, but good-humoredly and with a grin, saying things to that stubborn, sheep-like, complacent face that nobody else would dream of daring to say, and old Lindstrom would laugh and pretend to think he was joking. But presently he would do the thing Murray wanted him to do as if it had been his own idea all along.

It was by these tactics that Camilla's guardian rescued her and gave her the chance, which really was all she needed, for living a normally happy young girl's life. His friends, especially the women, laughed at him a good deal over the serious way in which he took his duties, but without producing the slightest effect. Nominally Camilla lived at home when she wasn't at school, but what with summer camps, vacation trips, one or two of them to Europe, Christmas holidays in the Adirondacks, and so on, she didn't average thirty days a year at Oak Ridge from her eleventh birthday to her nineteenth.

Murray spoiled her outrageously, of course. Miss Foster was quite right. Camilla could talk him into practically anything. And she was probably right, also, in considering that he was romantic about Camilla, or as she put it somewhat more tersely, "nuts"; though this was an aspect of the affair which he appeared unconscious of and would no doubt have denied with violence. He did recognize it as somewhat awkward that though arithmetically he was still twenty-five years older than Camilla, their relations were somewhat changing in character and getting rather complicated.

She was eighteen when her grandmother's death made room for a new disturbing element in the Oak

Ridge household, namely the Miss Parsons whose voice Miss Foster didn't like. Miss Parsons had been engaged a few months before the old lady's death as a sort of secretarial and companionable supplement to the nurse. On Mrs. Lindstrom's good days she wrote her few notes, read aloud to her and kept her amused. On the bad days, leaving the old lady to the nurse, she performed services of the same general sort for old Mr. Lindstrom himself, and so well did she succeed in pleasing him that when his wife died the old man would hear of nothing but that Miss Parsons should stay on living in the house as before.

The rest of the indoor staff comprised an elderly housekeeper, a cook and a maid. The outside people who didn't live in the house were a chauffeur and his wife, who was the laundress. They lived in a cottage down by the gate. The head gardener and his assistant lived off the place altogether, in two cottages up the road.

It was the last week in May that Mrs. Lindstrom died. Camilla came home from school for the funeral but went back to graduate without having been informed of her grandfather's decision to retain Miss Parsons' services for himself. But on the morning of commencement day she got a typewritten letter from her grandfather containing three pages of good advice and a check for five dollars as a commencement present. The check was made out in a woman's handwriting and the initials "L. P." were at the bottom of the letter.

When Murray had got off the train a little later that morning, having gone on to see her graduate, he'd found her waiting on the platform for him, and she'd hardly taken time to kiss him before producing this letter and pointing out the sinister implications she saw in it.

"'L. P.' is that Parsons woman, isn't it, Pete?" She'd adopted years ago the nickname his contemporaries called him by. "He's kept her on for his secretary, then, and let the man go? Is she living with him?"

"She's living in the house," Murray said, and he saw in the smile that flickered across her lips that she appreciated the distinction but didn't think it amounted to much. These sweet girl graduates of to-day knew more than they'd been taught, all right.

"What does 'L' stand for?" she wanted to know. "—Lucy?"

"Better than that," said Murray. "Lucretia."

"Lucretia Borgia," his ward commented bitterly. "Well," she went on, after a moment's reflection, "I suppose there really wasn't anything you could do about it. Except you might have let me know. Come along into the station and we'll telegraph for a berth for me. I'm going home with you."

They'd almost had a quarrel over that, for the plan had been that Camilla was to stay on three weeks longer to do some high-tension tutoring and take her college board examinations for Smith, and he couldn't assent to the impulsive kicking to pieces of a project as important as that without at least a protest.

He had of course seen for himself the possibilities inherent in the situation which Miss Parsons had so cleverly maneuvered herself into and he'd begun taking steps of his own to cope with her, but Camilla's lightning jump to the conclusion that the woman meant to marry her grandfather and get possession of all his money took him aback. It didn't strike him either that his ward would be a useful ally in his campaign.

"You settle down to your examinations and leave the Parsons woman to me," he had boldly advised Camilla. "I'll see that she doesn't slip anything over on us. I'm having her looked up, and if she starts anything I'll probably be able to bluff her out, or at worst, buy her off for a reasonable figure. There are no signs of anything sinister so far."

[24]

"You mean you haven't seen any," said Camilla. "But grandfather is afraid of you. You boss him around. And I'll bet she knows it. If they're planning anything funny, like a new will, they can get another lawyer, can't they? And if they were going to get married they wouldn't even have to do that. People are allowed to get married, aren't they, no matter how old and foolish they are? How soon is it legal after their first wife's dead?"

"One minute," said Murray absently. That suggestion of Camilla's that the old man might go behind his back troubled him a little but he tried not to let her see it. "But at that I don't see that there's anything for you to get in a sweat about. If she marries him her dower right is only a third of the estate, and God knows that will leaves enough for you and Eric; more than's good for either of you."

"It isn't that," she said hotly. "I've got enough money right now. But after all these years, after the life he led both mother and father, pinching and squeezing and never letting them call their souls their own, giving me five dollars for a commencement present, I'm not going to have him make a millionaire out of any damned blondined gold-digger. If he marries her I'll put arsenic in her soup. No, but really, Pete,

I'm going home, just as fast as I can get there. If you go home to-morrow and leave me flat I'll bum rides along the highway. I'm going home to get her job."

Judging by the immediate tangible results, it was probably, Murray reflected, a mistake to have given in. He had fairly talked himself hoarse during their trip west in the train, counseling caution and patience. "You'll have to treat Lucretia as if you liked her," he pointed out. "If you give her any sort of handle she'll grab it and use it against you with your grandfather for all it's worth. And for heaven's sake, don't try to hurry the old man. Just remember where you get your own stubbornness from: he's the original source of it. Yours is just a small negligible chip off the old block."

Camilla, grateful and perhaps even slightly penitent over the way she'd bullied him into letting her come home with him, promised to be good and patient and to keep her temper.

Nevertheless the explosion Murray feared had come off before she'd been three days at Oak Ridge. Her grandfather had seemed so glad to see her, she'd explained to Murray, and so pleased to learn that she'd given up her idea of going to college in order to come home and live with him, and besides, she'd been convinced that he was beginning to see for himself that the Parsons woman was poisonous, sly and bad-tempered and playing some game of her own, that she, Camilla, had been inspired to strike while the iron was hot and ask outright for the secretary's job. She'd seen at once from the look of sour suspicion her grandfather had turned upon her that this had been a mistake. But by that time she was in too deep to get out, so she'd gone on and spoken her mind and they'd had a terrific quarrel.

"You were perfectly right," she concluded, "and I was perfectly dumb to think I knew better than you and insist on having my own way. But all the same," she went on, after having paused a second or two to give this handsome admission time to take effect, "all the same, I'm glad I came home, and I'm almost glad I've quarreled with grandfather. Because now I'm going to learn to fly."

"Well, I'm dumber than you," Murray said bitterly. "I ought to have known this would happen if I ever let you come home. I ought to have strangled you in your beautiful raven hair while you were still an innocent child. Camilla, don't be half-witted! You know what your grandfather thinks about airplanes."

"I do," said Camilla. "I've been home four days."

Right across the river from the Lindstrom place was

a great flat two-hundred-acre field where they had opened this spring a new flying school and airport. The river, running sluggishly between low banks, was at no point between the Lindstrom place and the field more than fifty yards wide, and whenever the wind was due east or due west, planes took off or swooped to a landing right over his chimneys. Even when they were flying so high as to be almost inaudible the mere knowledge or suspicion that there were airplanes above his property turned him white with rage. He insured himself heavily against damage from them and probably lived, Murray thought, in the unacknowledged hope that one of them, a good big one, would crash some day through the roof of his greenhouse.

"You know, he might cut you off in his will for a trick like that," Murray told Camilla. "I mean it. He might make up his mind that it showed you were too light-headed and irresponsible to be entrusted with serious money. If he ever did, nothing could stop him and nothing could change him."

He thought he'd impressed her a little but as usual she came back with an argument. "The thing that made him so furious yesterday was suspecting that I'd come home to get the Parsons woman's job because I was thinking about his money. He might cut me out of his will for that. He hates to think that people are wondering how much they're going to get and when they're going to get it. So from that point of view probably the best thing I could do would be something like flying—just to show him I didn't give a damn.

"But that wasn't why I signed up for the course, Pete.—Yes, sure I did, and paid for it too, with your graduation present. I did it because I know it's what I have to do. I've known it for two years, really; ever since we flew together the first time from Berlin to Amsterdam. I've been thinking about it a lot. It will be the best education you can give me, Pete. Better than the whole four years at Smith would have been. I'll be a nicer girl, more reasonable and not so much trouble if you'll let me go through with it. And I don't see that grandfather and the Parsons woman have to find out anything about it; not until I've really learned and got my license, anyhow. I told them over at the field, when I signed up, that their press agent would have to lay off me and they agreed to it. I gave them your apartment for my address—you're my guardian, after all—so the mail will all come to you: little blue printed notices from the department of commerce; things like that."

Eventually he'd given in, of course, and in this matter he was inclined to think he'd been right. According to her instructor she was born to it, not only with the right instincts and good hands, but with a cool level head besides. She must get an enormous exhilaration out of it. You could see a sort of glow about her for an hour or two after she'd come back to earth. She'd asked him quite seriously one day if he didn't think she'd improved.

"You may not have noticed it so much but I'm sure grandfather has. I'm really nice to him now, and as for Lucretia Borgia, I'm simply saccharine tablets to her."

"It's good for people to be happy, I guess," was Murray's explanation.

But she thought there was more to it than that. "Miss Kittredge was always talking to us about discipline," she mused. "She said it was anything that forced your mind to think. If that's true, flying is a discipline all right. You see, the danger isn't the sort that it's fun to play with, like the danger of getting caught out of bounds by a house mistress, or even taking a spill riding a horse over a hurdle. The game is to make it as safe as you can, and to keep it safe you have to take it seriously. And I suppose," she concluded, "when you've really learned to be serious about one thing you sort of naturally stop being a damned fool about others."

Camilla was growing up, all right. The next thing he knew she'd be falling in love and marrying somebody. There was one of the pilots out at the field that he'd been wondering about a little.

As he drew near the Lindstrom place he somewhat imperiled the other traffic on the pike by trying to keep one eye on the sky. There were a number of student planes up taking advantage of the smooth air and the clear evening light. One of them might be Camilla's, though he wouldn't know it if he saw it. What he really hoped was that she would waylay him at the chauffeur's cottage down by the great iron gates, which were the only entrance to the place except from the river.

In the old days these gates had been matters of ornament more than anything else, but now, with the neighborhood what it was, with a filling station, a barbecue and a dance pavilion across the road, they had to be kept shut or casual intruders would have been swarming all over the place. That sort of trespassing couldn't be regarded as inexcusable, either. The ornate cupola, which was all you could see of the house from the entrance to the grounds, gave the place more the look of a public institution of some sort than of a dwelling.

Murray was surprised, however, to find the gates locked. That wasn't done as a rule until after dark, and it wouldn't be that for nearly an hour. He rang the gate bell and while he waited for an answer, speculated idly upon one of the new horrors of civilization that was just now assailing his ear. A big sedan which had pulled up for gas at the filling station directly across the road had a radio set in it, the loud speaker going full blast with the falsely infantile accents of some soprano which cut the still air like a knife. Later he was to wish very earnestly that he had employed that wait of a minute or more in observing his surroundings instead of reflecting upon them in a superior manner.

A little girl about ten came out of the chauffeur's cottage with the key, and if she at first struck Murray as rather young for a concierge her intensely efficient manner quickly changed his mind. She tugged the gate open, refusing his offer of help so indignantly that he did not press it. But this led to a good deal of conversation, as well as to a tip of ten cents before their little encounter ended. It appeared that she knew him and that this wasn't anywhere near all she knew. The

gate had been locked early because her father and
mother had gone out together, having told her not
to let any one in she didn't know. She knew Mr.
Murray, all right. He was Camilla's guardian. She
was sort of surprised that Camilla wasn't in the car
with him now, since she had been away from home
all day and hadn't got back yet. But maybe she'd gone
to meet her brother.

"Eric!" Murray was startled into exclaiming rather
loud. "Where's he?"

"Oh, he's coming home," she told him. "They got
a telegram from him to-day from California."

Probably she could have gone on telling him interesting facts for another ten minutes—her manner
suggested it, somehow—but there was a rather violent
recrudescence of the radio in the sedan across the road
just then which attracted her attention as worth in-
vestigating. So she accepted his tip in a perfectly
professional manner and let him go. There was a
lurking sense in his mind that he should have waited
to see that she locked the gate, especially since the
dime in her little palm was good for two ice-cream
cones, probably, at the barbecue stand across the road.
But, again to his subsequent deep regret, he ignored
this twinge of conscience.

[33]

The Lindstrom place, once you had gained admittance to it, had a certain beauty, with its well-kept lawns, its masses of shrubbery and the noble growth of elm and maple which the old man had planted when he built the house. Even the house had lost most of its ugliness under the veil of vines which had grown over it. Perhaps but for its tragic associations with the lonely half-demented woman who had lived most of her life here and with the murderous mania of her son it wouldn't even have been melancholy. In fact, most of the sense of its being melancholy would have been lifted from Pete Murray's mind by a glimpse of Camilla waiting about to share with him some of the exhilaration of her first flight in her own airplane; especially if she could have told him that that bright, pretty, but rather terrible, little girl at the gate had been mistaken about Eric's telegram.

The sudden return of this almost unkown wanderer was a little disturbing. What, just now, was he coming home for? What effect would his reappearance produce upon Camilla; upon her grandfather; and upon the somewhat enigmatic plans of the secretary? He thought he knew now, though, why he had been summoned and why Lucretia Borgia's voice had sounded so queer over the telephone.

CHAPTER II

STREAKS ON THE LAWN

MURRAY had had many a bad evening in this house (he once told Camilla that the only thing he ever enjoyed doing here was walking out the front door with her tucked under his arm) but this one, from the moment when Mrs. Smith, the housekeeper, opened the front door for him in a manner more than usually portentous, promised to be the worst, and kept its promise.

On his asking her pleasantly how she was, she began weeping large stony tears and told him she was leaving that night, directly after dinner in fact. She had had a telegram this afternoon that her son, James, in Salt Lake City was very ill and she was going to him. She added that nobody, no matter who he was, could keep her from doing her duty as a mother, not though it cost her her place. She raised her voice a little as she said this and Murray guessed that it was meant to reach the ears of somebody else, probably old Lindstrom himself around the corner in his study. And she then ushered Murray into the parlor and left him.

Miss Parsons wasn't looking in the least like Camilla's nickname for her when, a moment later, she came down-stairs and into the parlor to greet him. She looked wistful rather than wicked and Murray believed she really had been crying—and undoubtedly not over James. He'd have felt sorrier for her than he did if it hadn't occurred to him that with her skill at make-up she could have concealed the ravages of grief a lot better than she did, and that she meant to use them to make him sorry for her. Him or old Lindstrom. Had they been having a quarrel, then?

He thought she was on the point of speaking to him about it, for she came close and drew in her breath in a confidential sort of way, but the big clock in the hall boomed out one stroke just then for half past seven and she backed away from him. This was natural enough since they heard Mr. Lindstrom creak up out of his chair on the stroke and come limping toward them from his den, where he'd been waiting all this time to be punctual.

He was full of little inhuman affectations like that. He'd heard Murray come in of course, but it would have been against his principles to come out and greet a guest arriving two or three minutes ahead of time. His waxen face with its close-clipped, pointed, white beard was more than usually expressionless to-night, Murray thought, which probably meant that he, too, was troubled about something.

He greeted Murray with the formula that it was very good of him to have come, and then without even so much of a glance at Miss Parsons as would have acknowledged her presence in the room, he led the way to the dining-room, taking it for granted as he always did that dinner was ready the moment the hour had struck. Miss Parsons and Murray followed him. There was a fourth place set at the table for Camilla, and Murray, though he felt as he spoke that it was an indiscretion, asked where she was. Mr. Lindstrom ignored the question and Miss Parsons, after a silence, answered that she didn't know. "I suppose she'll come in late," she concluded. "She often does."

It was a ghastly dinner, all right, in spite of the good food. Mrs. Smith continued to act, according to her custom, as a sort of butler, supervising the activities of a rather pretty maid and impressively waiting on Mr. Lindstrom herself, but to-night her tragic air made her seem like an ancient prophetess of evil. Murray talked whenever he could think of anything impersonal to say but the other two scarcely pretended to second his efforts. The drum of an airplane overhead made him think of Camilla, but apparently it didn't suggest that association to her grandfather, which was a little something to the good.

Midway in the meal there occurred a minor incident which gave Murray something to think about. Mr. Lindstrom felt a draught, or thought he did, and asked Miss Parsons to go and find what was open. Murray offered to go in her place but forebore to insist when he saw she was glad of an excuse for a momentary escape from that room. She was gone a good deal longer than it would have taken her to find and close the window she reported as having been open in the study with a strong new breeze blowing through it, but it wasn't this that aroused Murray's curiosity. She had left the room dejected, limp, spiritless, and had returned to it in a curiously altered mood, with a kind of hard bright glitter about her, as if something had drawn up her nerves to the highest pitch, as if some crisis which she had long been expecting were immediately at hand.

Old Lindstrom, however, didn't seem to note this change in her and of course Murray refrained from commenting upon it. When the coffee came in she said she didn't want any and asked to be excused. Murray, listening with considerable interest, presently heard her light firm footsteps going up the stairs.

Then Mr. Lindstrom said, "Bring your coffee and your cigar into my study. We can talk there without being overheard."

This was a room Murray knew well. He'd spent endless hours here trying to bring the old gentleman's stubborn stagnant mind to necessary decisions of one sort or another. It was an incongruous room due to the conflict between poor Mrs. Lindstrom's attempt to make it homelike with her idea of comfortable sitting-room furniture and some rather pathetic decorations, pictures and so on, and her husband's desire for efficiency, which expressed itself in an uncompromising office desk and chair and steel filing cabinets. Its principal peculiarity was a narrow private staircase connecting it with the big bedroom overhead where old Lindstrom slept. It was solidly enclosed in paneling and had doors both at the top and at the bottom of it. There was a glass-fronted bookcase against one of the walls filled with sets of books uniformly bound in leather, and a safe occupied a special niche under the stair, its door masked by the paneling.

When the room door stood open upon the broad passage which ran right through the middle of the house the study was an extraordinarily good strategic point for keeping aware of what was going on. You could see into both the parlor and the sitting-room on the other side of the passage, you could hear every one who went up or came down either the front or the back stairs, and it would be impossible for any one to come in, either by the front door or the porte-cochére, without detection by a person on duty in this listening post. Its private staircase, too, enabled its owner to occupy it at any time in an unostentatious, not to say stealthy manner. When, however, its thick, well-fitted door into the passage was closed upon you you always began to think about being buried alive.

Old Lindstrom didn't begin immediately telling Murray what was on his mind even when the door was closed and they were both seated. Instead he began fumbling at his desk in an effort, Murray saw, to release the catch to the secret drawer. This was the sort of secret which might remain unsuspected by a casual incurious visitor, but which a thief would probably solve in two minutes. He pulled open the top drawer in the left-hand pedestal just the right distance and pressed a plunger in the side of it, which at that point released the catch. The secret drawer, a shallow tray the whole width of the well, with its front masked by the trim of the desk, slid open of itself, acted upon by springs when this catch was released. To lock it again you simply pushed it tight shut.

Murray had seen it opened scores of times, though the etiquette had always been that he pretend not to notice how the mechanism was operated. To-night, however, the old gentleman called his attention to it and carefully explained how it worked. "I tell you this," he then said, chipping his words out one at a time so that they fell like fragments of rock under the stone mason's chisel, "so that you will understand the very serious situation which I discovered this afternoon.

"I had left Miss Parsons here with certain duties which involved the use of the typewriter while I withdrew to my bedroom, which, as you probably know, is overhead. This window was open and so was mine, which enabled me very easily to hear the typewriter. After a little while, long before she could have finished her work, the noise of the machine stopped for so long a time as to attract my attention. Eventually I came down-stairs and opened that door. The woman was sitting here in my chair. When I came in upon her she sprang to her feet in a very guilty and suspicious manner. I took this chair myself and sent her back to her typing, and I made no investigation until she had finished her work and I had dismissed her for the afternoon. Then I made an examination, and found, as I suspected, that she had been rummaging in this secret drawer. The proof was easy. She had tried by leaning forward against the edge of the desk to press the drawer back into place but she had not pressed it far enough to catch."

"You're perfectly satisfied, I suppose," Murray suggested, "that you shut it yourself the last time you had it open?"

"I am more than satisfied," said Lindstrom, with dignity. "I am completely and absolutely certain."

Murray nodded. "Well, then, there's very little doubt she's been prying. What do you keep in the drawer? I take it there's nothing missing."

"No, there is nothing missing," the old man conceded, "—that is to say, nothing tangible is missing. But I strongly suspect that a secret is missing and is a secret no longer. I keep the combination of the safe in this drawer, Mr. Murray, and I believe the woman has memorized it."

"Good Lord," said Murray, "didn't she *know* the combination? Hadn't you ever given it to her?"

"Certainly not!" the old gentleman exclaimed. "Why should I do such an extraordinary thing?"

"As a matter of convenience, merely," Murray said soothingly. "Anyhow, assuming she knows it now, is there anything in the safe that would repay her investigation—or anything of intrinsic value?" He misunderstood the old man's blank look as springing from a failure to catch the meaning of the question. "—Your late wife's jewels, for example," he added.

"Intrinsic value!" Mr. Lindstrom exclaimed when he had got his breath. "I keep a fortune in that safe, sir. Not my wife's jewels—they're in a box at the bank—a fortune in money, twenty-five thousand dollars of United States gold certificates."

"Permanently?" Murray could hardly believe his ears. "Do you mind telling me why, at a cost to yourself of twelve or fifteen hundred dollars a year, you keep a sum of money like that where any second-class yegg with a bottle of nitroglycerin in his pocket could get it?"

"Yes, I will tell you why." The old man's wax-like cheeks were pink, but whether with pride or embarrassment Murray didn't know. "The beginning of my fortune was my having a sum like that in hand. That was the exact amount I had when my wife and I arrived in Chicago during the great fire. As soon as I had become rich enough to afford it I put an equal amount of money in that safe so that in case of another emergency I should be ready again. But you will understand," he concluded, while Murray sat staring at him speechless, "that if this woman is a thief, or the accomplice of a thief, there is something here, as you say, worth her trouble."

"I see that—yes," Murray agreed. "But I don't see what you're consulting me about. Whether she was actually prying or merely acting in a way to raise the suspicion that she was, the simplest thing to do is to dismiss her. You don't want my advice for that, surely?"

"Certainly not. My mind is already made up on that. The only reason I have not told her so, the only reason she is still in the house, is that I wished her detained here until I could secure your legal opinion as to whether it would be proper to have her arrested for breaking into my desk."

"I've never been asked for an easier opinion than that," Murray told him promptly, with a grin. "It would not only be improper, it would be ridiculous— embarrassingly ridiculous—and probably expensive into the bargain. By your own story she hasn't broken open your desk. She's merely unlocked the drawer in it. And you couldn't possibly prove to a jury that she'd done that. All you could offer as proof is your own assertion that you're sure you've never forgotten to lock the drawer yourself; yet the only apparent reason you can have for keeping a memorandum of the combination of the safe in that drawer is that you can't trust your memory for it. No, give Miss Parsons your blessing, Mr. Lindstrom, and let her go. Have them change the combination of the safe to-morrow if you like. There's nothing·actionable about that. Personally I don't believe she took the slightest interest in the combination of the safe. Don't you keep anything else in that drawer that she might have been curious about?"

"A personal letter now and then."

"Have you put one in recently?"

"Only this morning," the old man answered. "A letter from my grandson, Eric, which required no answer and was no concern of hers to read, so after I had read it myself I took the first occasion when she was out of the room to lock it away. She can have no possible interest in Eric, however. I will follow your advice and have the combination changed; also I will let Miss Parsons go without taking any further action. Thank you for your advice."

This of course was a clear dismissal, and, probably

because the advice had been unpalatable, he didn't soften it by rising or even by holding out his hand. Murray was used to his bad manners, however, wished him good night pleasantly enough and crossed over to the door.

He had his hand on the knob when he heard something queer that arrested his movement and held him for an instant rigidly attentive. It sounded like a cry of extreme surprise, or even of fear. It was faint, and yet it oddly seemed not to come from far away but rather as if it had been made right here in the room, only by a phonograph with a soft needle and the sound box muffled. He looked back at old Mr. Lindstrom. He apparently had heard nothing, and his ears were sharp enough, too.

Murray's pause, however, had given the old man time to get over his sulks and he now rose to say good night. "I'm sorry to say," he remarked, "that my grandson's letter informed me that he is coming home. I do not relish the idea of his living here: a very light-headed, foolish young man, unfit, I am sure, to be trusted with money. He has no sense of its value."

"He may have improved in the last ten years in that respect," Murray suggested.

"But he has not," old Lindstrom exclaimed. "Look

at this. This is a telegram that came from him to-day. More than forty words. A telegram; not a night-letter or even a day-letter. And it contains no necessary information that had not arrived here by mail before the telegram itself. Only a matter of a dollar or two, you say. But I say to you that the folly is the same as if it had been a matter of a thousand or two. And Camilla is as bad. I spent most of the working hours of this day drawing up a memorandum of instructions for you in regard to certain changes in my will. If Miss Parsons had not so seriously upset me I should have had it ready to show to you to-night. However, you shall have it in a day or two."

Only a very small corner of Murray's mind had been attentive to what old Lindstrom was saying about his will. This momumental and labyrinthine work had been keeping the office busy for years and it was doubt-ful if it would ever be completed to his satisfaction. But the telegram which the old gentleman had put into his hands aroused his lively curiosity.

He didn't wonder that it enraged the old gentleman. It told not only what train Eric was coming on and the day and hour when it was due to arrive in Chicago; it gave the name of the sleeping-car he was riding in and the letter of the drawing-room he occupied in it.

Beyond that it merely told, as apparently his letter had already done, that he was coming home either for a short visit or for good, as circumstances might dictate. If he had been ill and wanted to be sure of being met at the door of his drawing-room the moment his train pulled into the Chicago station such explicitness might be understandable. But this interpretation was contradicted by the sentence, "Do not meet me. I will taxi straight out to Oak Ridge." Was it pure folly, as the old man thought, or was there an intention buried in it too deep for Murray to find?

He was still hunting for the answer to this question when the old man gave a tug at the bell-pull to summon a servant to let his guest out of the house, said good night to Murray, and as soon as he had stepped out into the passage, closed the door after him, shutting himself into the study. He meant, no doubt, to go to his own room by the private stair. Murray, of course, was never to see him again alive.

He wouldn't have waited merely to be shown out ceremonially by a servant, but he did want to learn from some one in the household if Camilla had come in or if there was any news of her, so he stood still in the hall for a moment or two waiting for the bell to be answered. There was no sound of any one coming to answer; indeed the silence struck him as being just then rather thick, as if all the people in the house were simultaneously holding their breath, and his hearing sharpened itself accordingly.

The first faint sound he did hear startled him, the half-suppressed sniff or sob of some one trying to cry quietly. He thought of Camilla of course, though crying wasn't a thing she did very much, and walked swiftly around the foot of the stair into the corner of the hall where the sound came from. The person who turned from the window to face him was, however, not Camilla but Mrs. Smith, the housekeeper. She had her hat on and the presence of two big bulging valises and a number of smaller articles of luggage at her feet showed that she was only awaiting the arrival of some expected conveyance for making her final departure.

"I'm sorry to have startled you," Murray said, since it was so evident that he had. "I heard a sound and thought it might be Camilla."

"She hasn't come in yet," Mrs. Smith told him, "and she hasn't got a key, either. But I've told Sophy to listen for her. I can't wait much longer. If Mossop doesn't come for me pretty soon with his car I'll miss my train."

"I didn't know," Murray remarked, "that there was any train leaving for the west as late as this."

"It makes a stop at Oak Park," she said, "at half past eleven, and I'm going to catch it there."

Murray, not paying very close attention, had thought of something that might explain the odd sound he'd heard. "Did anything surprise you or frighten you so that you cried out just a few minutes ago?" he asked.

She said no and that she hadn't heard, either, any such sound as he described. She had been crying because she had been so terribly anxious about her son and worried lest she miss her train, but she hadn't made any noise about it.

She looked so pathetic and miserable that Murray said, "My car's right down here in the drive. If you like I'll run you and your luggage down to the gate and you can wait for Mossop there. That will save you some minutes." She was so grateful for the offer of this bit of help that it made him feel rather small not to offer to drive her all the way to Oak Park. It was only five miles or so. But he was by now seriously disturbed about Camilla, and it had occurred to him that he might get some information about her by applying at the airport. So he discharged his passenger and her voluminous luggage at the door of Nelson's cottage by the gate. She could leave in an hour and still make her train.

It was Nelson's wife, the laundress, a handsome Amazon of thirty, who came out to unlock the gate when she heard Murray's car in the drive. But she forgot all about him at sight of his passenger and her luggage, and on hearing of Mossop's failure to appear she summoned her husband to help her deal with the crisis. It wasn't advice she wanted, however, for she settled everything instantly herself. Mrs. Smith was to wait in the cottage—Fred would carry in the bags—until it was really time to start, and if Mossop hadn't come by then Fred himself would drive her to Oak Park in Mr. Lindstrom's Rolls-Royce. It was evident to Murray that Nelson was aghast at this idea, and equally evident that he would carry it out if necessary. It was he, as Murray recalled the next morning, who finally got the gate key from his wife and released Murray, who by this time was very impatient to be off.

Somehow, in the illogical way in which even a logical mind works when it is emotionally involved, he had from the moment he thought of applying for news at the airport been confident that they would have something completely reassuring to tell him. They'd know all about Camilla and be able to convince him that she was all right. So it was one of the worst shocks he'd ever had in his life to discover that the people at the port were as alarmed about her as he, and knew nothing beyond the fact that after half a dozen practise hops in her new ship with the instructor, she'd taken off alone at about six o'clock. She hadn't gas for more than two hours so she must have come down somewhere at least two hours ago, it being now ten o'clock. It was pretty hard to explain her not having telephoned, except on the theory of a crack-up.

As soon as he had brought himself to believe what they told him, Murray drove back to his apartment in town as fast as he could, miraculously without accident or arrest. If Camilla were able to telephone she'd telephone to him, and if not her pilot's license bore his address.

Having been told by his man that there was no news, he could think of nothing better to do than wait. He had left his car parked at the curb so that he could respond instantly to any summons, and without undressing beyond taking off his coat and loosening his collar he drew a chair to the open window, set the telephone at his elbow and began his vigil. By fits and starts he read mechanically every word of a long detective story, though very little of the contents of the printed pages actually reached his mind. He had some queer dreams too, though he was sufficiently awake to hear and count all the strokes, .quarters, halves and hours, of a clock somewhere in the neighborhood. The return of daylight made it harder to stay where he was and gave added strength to the crazy impulse to rush out and begin looking for Camilla at random.

It was a quarter after seven when the thrill of a bell startled him into snatching up his telephone. But it wasn't the telephone. The bell rang again while he held the instrument in his hand. His door-bell, then. He got unsteadily to his feet, his muscles not working very well somehow. But by rising he was able to see the street below his window and at the curb Camilla's car parked behind his own. No one but Camilla herself would have driven to his door in that car.

Lord, what a night she'd given him! He hoped, as he pressed the button releasing the latch to the vestibule door, that he could get himself together sufficiently by the time she'd run herself up in the little automatic elevator to give her the dressing down she deserved. He doubted it though. He couldn't stop trembling. He'd be lucky if he didn't burst into tears. That fantastic idea provided him with a sort of grin to greet her with as she opened the elevator door.

It must have been a pretty sick-looking one though, for after a momentary but very intent gaze at him in the insufficient light her own eyes filled with tears and she cried, "Oh, Pete, I'm so sorry! What a terrible night I must have given you!"

"The worst I ever sat through," he answered simply.

She led the way into his sitting-room. "In that chair?" she asked, noting the position of the telephone and the accumulation of perhaps half a hundred cigarette ends in the ash-tray.

"From about eleven o'clock last night until just now," he told her.

She gave her head a quick characteristic shake as of one dismissing an unprofitable feeling or memory, and grasping him firmly by both arms held him looking straight into her face. She spoke very deliberately. "I haven't been doing anything silly or reckless, Pete, or trying to show off. I haven't done anything since seven o'clock last night that wasn't the only thing I could do. If you won't believe that, Pete, I'll never fly again."

It was exactly like Camilla, coming into action, horse, foot and dragoons like that, and yet he knew it wasn't a calculated effect. "Of course I believe you," he said.

Whereupon she kissed him briefly and her manner lightened a little. "Well, this is what happened," she said. "See if you can think of anything better to have done than what I did.

"When I took off by myself I flew west a little way, to within sight of the Rock River, not making very good time because I was flying into the wind. I was counting on a tail wind to bring me home in no time. I saw a little amateur landing field beside a road with a filling station and a wind sock on a pole and I came down for a look at it.

"Then I noticed that the wind had changed and was blowing from the east. I didn't know whether I'd have gas enough to bring me back or not so I put the ship down to refuel. It took quite a while because the man in charge of the filling station wasn't used to having airplanes come in and was quite excited about it and wanted to be shown everything. I got filled up at last though, and took off and struck out straight for home.

"The fog caught me before I'd been up five minutes. It must have been coming along all the time on the east wind but I hadn't seen it when I was going the other way. It was all over the valley too, not just streaks as I thought it would be at first. I flew for about half an hour before I found a hole to come down through. I did find a hole and a ceiling about two hundred feet high, enough to clear the tops of trees and things but nowhere near enough to be comfortable. So I put the ship down again in the first likely-looking field I saw.

"It was a big forty-acre pasture with a whole herd of cows in it, Pete, and not a house in sight. Nobody had seen me come down, either, so there wasn't anything to do but stay there. It was almost dark then and it got darker than the inside of your hat. It wasn't as long a night as yours, I guess, because I didn't know that you knew I was out, but it was long enough.

"By and by the light came back and the sun came up and the wind blew off the fog and I took off, without hitting a cow, and flew back to the port. I got there about half past six; half past five, that is, by grandfather's clock, and an hour, anyway, before I could get into the house. I'd have telephoned you from the airport, of course, if I hadn't thought you'd still be asleep. So I jumped into the little car and came—in person."

"That sounds pretty good to me," he said. "All I don't see is why, when you found you were down for the night, you didn't hunt up a house with a telephone and call the airport."

"I was afraid to," she told him, "on account of the cows."

He started a wild sort of laugh but she checked it. "Not afraid for me, idiot," she said, "but afraid for the airplane. Don't you know," she went on to explain, "that cows adore. airplanes. They lick the dope off the fabric every chance they can get. I spent the whole beastly night heaving rocks at them to chase them away. Pete, why are you looking at me like that? Don't you believe I'm telling the truth?"

"I believe every word of it, darling," he assured her. "It's merely one of those stories that is intrinsically incredible. Thank heaven you don't need an alibi for last night!"

He said it as a joke but as he heard the spoken words he felt, as it were, a cold breath blow over him, and if she'd been looking at him she no doubt would have asked again what made him look so queer.

She had turned away though for a long shuddering yawn and stretch. "Get a bath and a shave and dress for another day, Pete, and let me tidy up a bit in your other bathroom. Only hurry. And tell your man to get me an enormous breakfast. I feel as if I could eat a dozen eggs. After that we'll figure out how you're going to square me with grandfather."

The oddity of their having breakfast alone together up here in his apartment and the relief they both felt from the anxieties of last night might have been expected to induce a mood of gaiety in both of them, but somehow or other this failed to appear. He started telling as lightly as he could the story of his evening's experiences but didn't get far with it, for his description of the terribly well informed little girl who had unlocked the gate led directly to her knowledge of Eric's telegram and this, it seemed, was absolutely news to Camilla. She fell into a brown study over it and lost her appetite, although the enormous breakfast she had said she was starving for was not half eaten.

"It's funny to have a real brother that you practically don't know at all—and to have him coming home, perhaps to live with you, in just a couple of days. I don't think I like it, Pete. It's sort of—scary."

"You'll find you know him better than that when you've thought about him a little more. You were eleven when he went away."

"All I can remember," she persisted gloomily, "is that I didn't like him and that I spent most of my time keeping out of his way. He didn't like me, either."

"I remember him as an unpleasantly self-centered young cub," Murray admitted, "but you'll probably find that he's improved with the passage of the years. Most people do—fortunately."

Camilla responded to this insult rather absently. "Even if he's nice," she said, "I don't think I want a brother. You're all the relatives I need. Rolled into one, you know, like the mate of the Nancy brig."

This joke wasn't very successful either. They went ahead with their breakfast in silence for a minute or two, a mere pretense on Camilla's part, Murray noted, as well as on his own.

Presently he looked at his watch. "Look here," he said, "it's quarter past eight, quarter past seven at Oak Ridge. If we drive out there now we'll find the old gentleman at his breakfast, which is when he's nearest human, I understand. We'll walk in on him and tell him what you've been up to, the whole story—down to the cows last night. Maybe he won't take it as hard as he would if he weren't already in a stew about Miss Parsons and Eric."

Soberly she agreed. "I don't care much how he takes it," she said, "as long as we get it over with. You'd better let me drive you out in my car; it'll be quicker."

"Well, there's one thing about your driving," he

observed when, after a dozen triumphs of hair's breadth steering and timing, she emerged from the clotted traffic of the town into the comparatively open streak of the highway. "It always serves to take my mind off my troubles."

She didn't taunt him with his middle-aged fears, or even smile. Evidently her mood was as sober as his own and neither of them spoke again until she pulled up at the gateway to her grandfather's place. Here, however, an astonishing phenomenon caused them both to exclaim in the same breath. The iron gates were standing wide open and no one, even though Camilla sounded her horn as she turned into the drive, appeared from the chauffeur's cottage. For the moment, at least, it seemed to be deserted.

"There goes somebody's job," said Camilla, "if grandfather ever hears about it." Then with a quick look at Murray she went on, "Do you think there's something wrong, Pete?"

"Yes," he told her, "I've got a hunch there is."

But she didn't respond to this as he had expected, with a spurt of speed. Instead she took her foot off the accelerator and let the car roll idly along the curves of the graveled drive. Presently at the point where the trees and shrubbery opened out to give them a view of a great expanse of lawn she clutched his arm. "Look over there, Pete! More trouble!"

Following the direction of her nod he saw three parallel streaks or tracks wide apart in the grass.

"Some idiot from the field has put a ship down here and taken off again. Let's hope it dries out before grandfather gets a look at it."

Another curve of the drive brought them in sight of the house, and guessing suddenly the significance of what he saw, Murray said sharply, "Let me out here, Camilla, and then drive around the circle and beat it back to town. Go to my apartment and stay there until I send for you. This is no place for you this morning."

All he had seen to bring him to the instantaneous conviction that this old house was once more a scene of tragedy and horror was a step-ladder standing on the grass outside the study window, the screen pushed up two feet or more, and a little girl, his acquaintance of the night before no doubt, standing on the ladder with her nose pressed against the glass.

Camilla patted his knee but drove steadily on. "It's no good, Pete," she said. "You can't keep me out of it now. Look, the police are here already."

What she nodded to was a blue motorcycle with a

side-car which had been trundled on to the grass beyond the veranda steps, and as she spoke the front door opened and a gaitered policeman came out, at the sound of their tires on the gravel, no doubt.

"Do you belong here?" he asked. "Have you any business here?" His manner was crisp but not discourteous.

"Miss Lindstrom lives here," Murray told him, pleasantly. "I'm Mr. Lindstrom's lawyer and her guardian. Will you tell us, please, what's happened?"

He looked intently at Camilla and seemed to hesitate to answer, so that she cried out, "Don't try to break it gently. Has something terrible happened to grandfather?"

He answered, "It looks as if he'd been murdered. Anyway, he's been shot." Neither of them spoke, and, again after hesitating a moment, he added, "I guess you'd better wait right here till the Chief's ready to talk to you. He's busy right now—only got here a few minutes ago—but he'll want you to tell him all you know about it, of course." Then he went in and shut the door behind him.

A look into Camilla's bloodless face and horrified eyes made Murray say quickly, "Sit down, Camilla!" She obeyed like a somnambulist and he seated himself

[62]

on the step beside her. When he heard a stifled sob from her and saw the tears running down her face he got out his handkerchief and handed it to her.

"I'm not crying because I loved him," she said. "I didn't. Nobody did. Nobody in the world. I suppose that's why I'm crying. But Pete, who *could* have killed him, an old old man like that?"

"We'll probably know in a very few minutes," he said. "Don't think about it. Try not to think at all."

But he couldn't follow his own advice. He was thinking of Camilla's story of her last night's adventure and wondering whether the policeman had seen that track of an airplane on the lawn.

CHAPTER III

ONE of those indescribable but expressive sounds
capable of being uttered through the human nose interrupted Murray's attempt to comfort Camilla. He looked
where it came from and saw the chauffeur's child gazing at them from across the drive, with a very sophis-
ticated and somewhat contemptuous expression. She
seemed to feel they were wasting their opportunities.

"You can go up the ladder now if you like," she
observed, "and look in the window. You can see his
legs from there pretty well but you can't see his head
nor any of the blood."

She seemed a perfectly monstrous little creature to
the bachelor Murray, enjoying these horrors the way
his idea of a normal child should enjoy its morning
orange juice and oatmeal. But her presence had the
tonic effect of rousing Camilla from her daze. "Whose
legs?" she asked.

"Why, your grandfather's," cried the child. "Don't
you know anything about what's been happening out
here at all?"

"Not much," Camilla admitted. "We just got here, you see. How much do you know?"

"Well, I guess I know just about as much as any one," the child answered smugly, "even if they wouldn't let me go in there and see the blood. I'll tell you all about it, shall I?"

"Yes," said Camilla, "come over here and tell us." She crossed the drive and scrambled to a seat on the top of one of the brick piers that flanked the steps. "We were having breakfast," she began, "down at our house, of course. You know where we live," she threw in parenthetically to Murray, "because I unlocked the gate for you last night. Well, the key's lost and my father and mother were having a quarrel about whose fault it was, so they didn't notice what was happening. But I was looking out of the window and I saw Sophy running as fast as she could run and crying and looking scared. She was coming to our house, so I opened the front door and went out to meet her and ask her what the matter was. She didn't pay any attention to me but went right in and began telling father and mother about it. They sent me out to play but I listened under the window and heard everything they said."

"I haven't," said Murray, deeply moved, "the slightest doubt of it." But Camilla laid her hand on his knee

to silence him and asked what it was that had frightened
Sophy.

"Well, you see," the child resumed, "Sophy and the
cook had had breakfast ready a long time and nobody
came down to eat it. So Sophy went up to call Miss
Parsons, because there wasn't any reason why *she*
should lie abed all day, and she found Miss Parsons
gone. Her bed hadn't been slept in and her things
were all slung around, as if she'd packed in a terrible
hurry. But she couldn't have taken much of her stuff
because most of it was left. So Sophy went down and
told the cook and they decided to call Mr. Lindstrom,
because he scarcely ever slept late like that anyhow.
Well, Sophy went back and knocked on his bedroom
door and he didn't answer, and then she went down and
knocked on the door to the study because he might have
gone down there by his inside stair. But of course
he didn't answer from there either. Then she began
to be frightened and went and got the cook, and they
tried both doors and they both were locked. So then
she came running as fast as she could down to our
house to get father."

This must, Murray thought, exhaust the child's useful information and he began fishing in his pocket for
another ten cents to dismiss her with when Camilla

asked another question. "What did your father do when Sophy had told him that much?"

"Well, Sophy was crying so hard she couldn't talk any more, so mother said for her to stay and have a cup of coffee and get quieted down while father went up to the big house and broke open the door. And father said all right but he'd have to go to the tool-house to get a wrecking bar. I waited for him to get a head start and then I followed him, and when he saw me and told me to go back we were pretty near the house, and I showed him how the screen to the study window had been pushed up and stuck, as if somebody had got in that way. So then he let me go along with him to the tool-house to carry the wrecking bar while he carried the step-ladder.

"He wouldn't let me look in, though," she went on in an aggrieved tone. "He said the window was locked and he'd have to get in the other way after all, and he made me come into the house with him and wait in the hall while he pried open the door. Mrs. Rosnes— she's the cook, you know—was there too, and she went in with him, but she gave a scream and came right out as soon as she saw the blood. She sent me home too, but I didn't go until I heard my father telephoning for the police. Then I went down to the gate to see them come. I thought they'd come in a patrol-wagon but they didn't; they came in that thing. Mother let them in the gate. It was locked with a padlock and chain because of the key being lost. And then she and Sophy came running up here after them. They didn't see me because . . ."

At this point the child's apparently inexhaustible flow of narrative did run dry, the instantly apparent cause of the stoppage being the opening of the front door and the appearance of her father on the veranda. Murray looked around at him in time to see a rather startled look come into his face as the significance of the tableau broke over him.

"I hope," he said, "my little girl hasn't been making a nuisance of herself."

"Not a bit," Camilla assured him. "She's been telling us all that's happened this morning."

He still, Murray noted, looked rather disturbed. He curtly ordered the child to go home and didn't say anything further to them until she had obeyed, at least to the extent of withdrawing sulkily out of sight around the first curve of the drive.

"I'm glad you've come, sir," he then said to Murray. "I tried to telephone you as soon as I called the police but your man told me that you and Miss Camilla had just left. This is a terrible thing that's happened," he went on. "It's a horrible sight to see an old man like that shot through the head. It's strange to think that a woman should do such a thing. This new Chief of Police, they say he's been to college and all that, but I'm afraid . . ."

"Have you been talking to him?" Camilla broke in.

"He didn't give me much chance to talk to him, Miss; asked a few questions and pulled me up very short on my answers, and then said he was through with me for the present. He's got Sophy talking to him now in the dining-room."

"I think before he sends for you again," Murray said, "you'd better go back and close the gate. It was standing wide open when we drove through."

"Yes, sir," Nelson said. "I'm very sorry, sir. I suppose in her excitement my wife forgot to close it after the police came. I hope Mr. Lindstrom won't . . ."

"No, he won't find out about it, Nelson," Murray said, "but at any rate, I'd go back now and close the gate." Even the sight of the old man dead hadn't sufficed at once to do away with the fear that he had inspired so long.

"We were all like that," said Camilla soberly. "We might not act afraid, but we were."

The policeman came out on the porch just then and told Murray that the Chief wanted him in the dining-room.

"Can't I come along too?" Camilla asked forlornly. Murray forestalled the policeman's refusal. "It'll be much easier for him to talk to us one at a time," he said, and left her sitting there with her face buried in her hands. She was in for a terrible day, poor child.

However, the Chief's manners were reassuring. He got up when Murray entered the room and introduced himself. "My name's Hopkins. I'm the new Oak Ridge Chief of Police—a little too new for comfort in a case like this. I'll be glad of all the help you can give me. Of course, the first thing I want is a description of the missing secretary."

Murray described her as well as he could, though there wasn't much to distinguish her by except the somewhat aggressive blondeness of her hair.

"What was she wearing?" the Chief asked. "I understand you dined here last night."

"I can't possibly tell you what she wore," said Murray, "except that she looked rather limp and pathetic in it. It was the sort of thin dress that a woman puts on to dine in on a warm evening when she isn't going out."

"Do you know anything that would help to trace her? What her references were when she got the job? I understand she's been here about a year."

"So far as I know," said Murray, "—and I made a point of trying to find out—she offered no references whatever. Mrs. Lindstrom engaged her and the person who brought it about was Mossop, the head gardener. He's an Englishman and she professed to be a compatriot of his as well as a devotee of gardens. When she succeeded in convincing him that both these professions were true, he showed her his garden, of which he is justly proud, and introduced her to Mrs. Lindstrom. She appears to have done the rest, unaided. She never volunteered any information to me about herself and a month or more ago I took steps to have her past looked into. So far, no results have come in."

"What led you to start the inquiry?"

"I wasn't perfectly sure what her intentions toward my client might be. Mr. Lindstrom was eighty-four and she was a very attractive and competent young woman."

"Pathetic, I think you said," remarked the Chief.

"Last night," Murray amended. "It wasn't her usual manner. Mr. Lindstrom had had a falling out with her in the afternoon and was on the point of dismissing her. It was in connection with that affair that he sent for me. I think I'd better tell you the whole story."

The Chief nodded, and Murray, as briefly as he could, went through the incidents of the evening. How Miss Parsons had left the dinner table to find the source of the draught that was blowing on Mr. Lindstrom; the curious change in her mood which Murray had noted when she returned; the story of the secret drawer and the legal opinion the old gentleman had wanted as to whether or not he could have the girl arrested

So far, the Chief listened without interruption but when Murray told him of the queer noise he had heard—a noise surprising enough to have frozen him for a moment where he stood with his hand on the door-knob, although Mr. Lindstrom sitting not ten feet away had apparently not heard it at all—the Chief got up out of his chair.

"I have been leaving that room undisturbed as far as possible until some people I have sent for get here. But I want you to come in and show me just where you stood and what direction, if you can remember, the sound came from."

He led the way down the hall, pushed open the door

which evidently wouldn't latch since Nelson had forced it with his wrecking bar and ushered Murray in upon the scene of the tragedy with the warning, "Don't touch anything." The warning wasn't needed for Murray had stopped in his tracks.

"I was standing right here," he said, "with my hand on the door-knob. I had said good night and was in the act of turning the knob when I heard the noise."

"You said it sounded as if it had been made right in the room itself," Hopkins reminded him. "What part of the room? Can you remember that?"

"It must have come in my right ear," Murray told him. "I remember turning my head this way."

While the Chief studied the floor, the walls, and the pictures in the corner he had indicated, Murray took a general look around the room. The old gentleman's body was lying on the floor just as Nelson had found it, on its back, the head toward the door to the private staircase and about far enough from it, Murray noted, to allow the door to clear it if it should be swung open. He doubted, though, if the old man had fallen as straight as that and from the appearance of the clothing he suspected that he had been dragged, a little way at least, by the feet. The head hadn't been shattered by the shot. There was a pool of blood beneath it, though not as much as Murray would have expected. The wound where the bullet had entered was beneath the right eye. The sight was ghastly enough to cause him to look away from it hastily. The rest of the room—and there was something horrifying about this observation too—looked exactly as it had last night.

"So far as I know," he said to Hopkins, "I'm the last person known to have seen him alive. Do you know of any one else who saw him after I left?"

The policeman shook his head. He was in the act of pulling on a pair of white cotton gloves, but he paused to smile at Murray as he said, "Still I don't suspect you at present of having murdered him." Then he explained what he wanted the gloves for.

"I'm going to see whether there's a wall ventilator behind any one of these pictures."

The one he began with was a small framed etching which hung head high to the right of the door. He uttered an exclamation of surprise as the picture came away, for there, projecting through the wall behind it, half an inch beyond its surface perhaps, was a tin tube about an inch in diameter.

"What the devil do you suppose that is?"

"A speaking-tube," said Murray instantly. "This

house was built before the days of electric bells and the walls are probably full of them. It had a mouthpiece on it, of course, when it was in use, with a cap that closed with a spring."

"That's where your noise came from, all right," said the Chief. "As soon as we know which room this particular tube leads to, we'll have a pretty good idea who made it; probably the secretary's room, I'd say. She was listening and she cried out over the old man's idea of having her arrested."

Murray shook his head. "It wasn't timed like that," he objected. "I had already told him he couldn't do that, explained why and got up to say good night after he'd dismissed me. Besides, I don't believe the tube goes to her room. I think you will find it goes to his, which is right above this. Otherwise, he'd have had it stopped up. He never would have allowed a perfect implement for eavesdropping in this room unless he meant to use it himself. The other thing I am pretty certain of is that the person who uttered that cry was surprised by something that happened in the room where she was and not by anything she heard down here."

"I'm expecting the coroner's people here any minute," the Chief remarked, uncertainly, "and Ballard, that new expert in ballistics and so on that they've got down at the university, is coming out in the course of the morning; so I've thought it better to keep the field clear as far as possible. But in the light of what you've told me, and the discovery of that speaking-tube, I think we'll have a look at that room up-stairs. We can just about open that door without moving him."

It had already struck Murray that this might be rather more than a coincidence and the surmise prepared him, to some extent, for the discovery that came an instant later.

The Chief unlatched the door, without touching the knob, by twisting the shaft between a powerful finger and thumb and, standing to the left of the body, watched as he slowly pulled the door open, to see that it was going to clear. So it happened that Murray got the first glimpse of what was behind the door and realized that this, and not the study, was the place where Mr. Lindstrom had been murdered. The stair ran up to the right, inside the paneling and parallel to it. A small square landing at the foot of the stairs, one step up, was what the door opened upon. It was carpeted, as were the stairs, and this carpet was sodden with blood. There were splashes and spots of blood, too, on the white plastered wall, to the left of the door and opposite the foot of the stairs. Four feet or so above the level of the landing was a broken spot in the plaster with a small hole in the middle of it, evidently the bullet hole.

The Chief, after a swift look into Murray's face, came around the body and stood beside him. "That bears you out," he said quietly. "She was in his room and shot him as he started up the stairs. But would she have dragged him out? Was she strong enough to have done it?" Without waiting for an answer to either of these questions, he started up the stairs and Murray followed him.

The bedroom was very dark and the Chief's first act was to walk to the nearest of the windows, draw back the curtains, and run up the blind.

Murray stopped to take his first general look at the apartment from the doorway. He had never been in the room before and the mere atmosphere of it interested him. The major articles of furniture, bed, bureau, wash-stand, and dressing-table, might easily have been, he thought, an exhibit at the Philadelphia Centennial. The enormous size and weight of the pieces, and the reckless determination to cover their entire surfaces with ornamental wood-carving, belonged, at least, to that period. The monstrous bed, with its canopy and its green velvet curtains, looked like an attempted assertion of royalty, but only half convinced. Had old Mr. Lindstrom derived a comforting sense of his importance from lying in it?

The Chief was drawing the curtains at the other window now and the light was better.

"This room has been ransacked, I think," he said, his gaze resting on the bureau which stood between the two big windows. "These drawers have been pulled out and slammed to in a hurry. They are all jammed."

Murray wasn't looking at the bureau but at the bed. The curtain which hung from the canopy on the side nearest him was festooned back in what was evidently its customary position. But the loop of the other curtain had come unfastened so that it fell in straight folds and not in natural folds either. They had a tight, strained look as if something lying on the floor beyond the bed were holding them.

"Look over there, Chief," Murray said.

Hopkins whirled around. From his position he could see what was holding the curtain down. He didn't cry out or utter any exclamatory sound but Murray saw his eyes widen and the muscle of his jaw knot.

"Come around and tell me if this is the missing secretary," he said.

It was indeed poor Lucretia. Whatever her schemes had been they had gone fatally awry. She lay on the floor, parallel to the bed and so close as to be almost under it, her feet tangled in the bed curtains, her head toward the foot of it. The pistol which had fired the fatal bullet must have been held within a few inches of her face, so blackened was it by the powder.

"Is that the dress she wore at dinner?" the Chief asked when Murray had identified her. "I remember you said you couldn't describe it."

"I recognize it, though," Murray told him. "She didn't change and that means, I take it, that she had no intention of leaving the house last night."

The Chief stooped down and shot a gleam from his flash-light under the bed.

"There's the gun she did it with," he said, and Murray, stooping, saw it too. He straightened up suddenly, without speaking, and walked away to the window.

"Too much for you?" the Chief asked. "Well, I don't wonder. But the situation is beginning to clear up, I guess. She was up here in this room looking for something—something, I suppose, she hadn't been able to find in the study earlier in the day—when she heard him coming up the stairs. She was in a panic over being caught the second time and she let him have it. Then she shot herself because it was the only thing left for her to do. I don't know that that covers all the ground, but it comes closer to it than any explanation we've found so far."

Murray made no comment and the Chief turned around for a look at him.

"You'd better go outside and get a breath of fresh air," he observed. "You're looking pretty sick. Don't leave the place, though. I shall want you on hand when the experts get here."

He opened the door—the locked door—into the hall as he spoke, turning the key and the knob by twisting their shafts just as he had done before, and Murray started away, rather unsteadily, in the direction of the front stairs. But before he had gone far, the Chief called after him, "How about Miss Lindstrom? Shall I talk to her? Can she add anything to what you've told me?"

"She was away from home last night," Murray said, "and most of yesterday. I brought her back with me only a few minutes ago."

"Then I won't trouble her at present," the Chief decided. "You'll see that she's on hand, of course, when I do want her?"

Murray nodded and went on down-stairs. But he paused a moment to pull himself together before going out on the porch to rejoin Camilla. It didn't matter— it could have no possible significance at all—that he had recognized the weapon illuminated by the Chief's flash-light under the bed as a target pistol he had given her two summers ago, when he was teaching her to shoot.

Chapter IV

LOST AND FOUND

Evidently his pause did not serve his purpose since Camilla, the moment she sighted him, cried out, "What is it, Pete? What's happened that's worse than what I know?"

He sat down beside her and laid what he hoped would be a steadying hand—although it was rather tremulous—on her knee. "They were wrong in thinking Lucretia had run away," he said. "We've just found her."

"Dead?" she asked. And, at his nod, "Murdered like grandfather?"

"Shot through the head as he was," he told her, speaking low. "We just this instant found the body up in his room, inside the locked door, dressed as she was last night at dinner. The Chief's under the impression that she shot him and then killed herself. But he can't hold that opinion long."

"Why not?" Camilla asked. "Why mightn't that be what happened?"

"Too many things contradict it. The revolver isn't

lying in the right place. It's near her right hand but it couldn't possibly have fallen there when she fell. Then, there's the position of the old man's body. He was shot on the private staircase and then dragged by the feet out into the study. She never would have done that. She could have had no purpose in doing it and then in going up-stairs again to shoot herself in his bedroom. Besides, I've got reason to believe that some one got into the house while we were at dinner. Your grandfather felt a sudden draught blowing on him and sent her from the table to find it and shut the window it came from. She came back looking different. Queerly excited. I think she found some one she knew, some intruder in the house, and hid him somewhere until she could go back and interview him at leisure. That would account for a good many queer things one way and another."

"What things?" she asked.

"There's something else I want to talk about first. Camilla, I think I recognized the pistol."

"Recognized?"

Her eyes widened as they stared into his face. "You don't mean it was my pistol, Pete? The one grandfather took away from me and hid?"

"That's what he did, is it? Yes, that's the one."

"Did you tell the Chief whose it was?"

He shook his head. "Perhaps I was wrong not to but I wasn't sure."

She rose swiftly to her feet and squared back her shoulders. "Come along," she said. "The sooner we tell him the better."

When Camilla flared up like that you didn't argue with her. You either stopped her by force or followed along, and the latter was what he did; across the hall, up the stairs and down the passage to where an open door and the sound of voices led them to the presence of the Chief. This was Lucretia's room where Hopkins was once more interrogating Sophy.

"Then, the room looks now just the way it did when you came up to call her for breakfast?"

"Yes, sir."

"Drawers pulled out like this? Closet door standing open?"

Sophy faltered a negative to this. She herself had looked in the drawers and opened the closet door to find out whether Miss Parsons had packed up and left for good.

"Did *you* sit down on the bed?"

Some one had, you could see plainly enough.

"No, sir," she said, "I didn't do anything like that.

I just took a quick look and went right down and told the cook about it."

"Well, I don't wonder you thought she'd bolted."

Sophy was a smart girl. She caught the implication and cried out, "You mean she hasn't gone? She's still here?"

"We know where she is, all right," the Chief told her. "Now run along. I don't want to ask you any more questions just now." He had glanced around quickly enough to see that this development hadn't surprised Camilla and he said in a low tone to Murray, "You've told her, then?"

Simultaneously with Murray's nod Camilla spoke for herself, reaching out for his hand, as if to hold him quiet, as she did so.

"Pete thinks he recognized the pistol," she said. "He thinks it's one he gave me for target shooting two summers ago. If you'll let me see it, I can tell you for sure whether it's mine or not."

"I don't want to disturb it at present," said the Chief. "You might look in the place where you keep yours and see whether it's there or not."

"It won't be there," she told him. "I only had it a little while and then grandfather took it away and hid it somewhere."

"You're sure it wasn't Miss Parsons who took it?"

"No, it was long before she came. And besides, grandfather told me he had taken it and locked it up."

"Did you tell any one that he had taken it? Mr. Murray here, for instance?"

"No," she said, "I was going back to school just about then and I forgot all about it."

"So far as I can see," remarked the Chief, turning back to Murray, after thinking this over for a minute, "that fits in with the theory that the Parsons woman did all the shooting herself. He probably kept the gun in the secret drawer to his desk and she found it there yesterday afternoon when she had the drawer open. Anyhow, I can't see any other theory that fits as well with the facts as we now know them. Both windows to the study were locked and are still and both doors were locked, this one up-stairs into his bedroom and the study door down-stairs into the hall. She was eavesdropping on your conversation with Mr. Lindstrom last night; knew she had been caught prying and was going to be dismissed for it. So she quarreled with him and killed him in the course of the quarrel."

He must have seen that Murray didn't agree with him for he added on a note of concession.

"That story doesn't cover the condition this room is in. She never would have torn it up herself this way and so far as I know now, there isn't any one else in the household who would be likely to do it." He turned upon Camilla. "Have you any suggestion to make on that score?" he asked.

She flushed at the suddenness of the question and hesitated, and he, not apparently having meant to rattle her, added explanatorily, "I mean on general principles, not with special reference to last night, since I understand you weren't at home."

"No," Camilla said, "I was out all night,"—a phrase which struck Pete as unfortunate and certainly drew an intent look from Hopkins. But Camilla went on steadily enough. "Why, none of us liked her very much, and I think we were all sort of suspicious of her. I know I was. I thought she was trying to slip something over on grandfather. Well, like marrying him, you know. But I never would have thought of searching her room and I can't see why any of the servants should have thought of it, either. I don't believe any of them did."

"You think the whole thing is an outside job, then?" Hopkins asked.

Murray wished the question had been addressed to

him. The Chief seemed to be coming into focus on Camilla in a way that made him uneasy.

"Why, yes, I guess so," said Camilla, uncertainly.

"Offhand," said the Chief, "the probabilities are against an outside job. Here's a place surrounded by a high wall, the only entrance being a gate, locked at night, and with some trustworthy person on duty all the time. Of course, that doesn't mean that an intruder couldn't have got in but it makes it more or less unlikely that one did."

Camilla drew a long breath and squared her shoulders.

"One intruder did get in late last night or early this morning," she said. "An airplane landed on the lawn and took off again while there was dew on the grass. Didn't you see the tracks? Pete and I did, anyway. I suppose they've dried out by now."

"I might have seen them all right," said Hopkins, "since I came down the drive not half an hour before you."

The words were spoken casually enough, but there was an implication in them, perhaps intentional and perhaps not, which made Pete uneasier than ever. Was the Chief pointing out to Camilla that she could claim no credit for telling him something he had had such

[88]

an excellent opportunity of discovering for himself?

Hopkins did not pause to stress the point, however. He went almost straight on still speaking casually. "You'd been away from home, I understand, since yesterday morning. I don't think Mr. Murray told me where you were."

"No," said Camilla, "I don't suppose he did. Of course he doesn't know except that he believes what I told him."

She looked at Murray, a woebegone smile on her lips, and asked, "Do you remember what you said when I'd finished telling you about last night?"

"I told you what was true," said Murray, "that I believed every word of it."

Camilla nodded and turned back to Hopkins. "But he said," she went on, "that it was lucky I didn't need an alibi for last night."

Was the girl trying, Murray wondered despairingly, to make the man think she had committed this appalling crime? She told the story much as she had told it to him earlier that morning, concisely, without explanatory elaboration, and yet without the omission of any significant detail. At the end of it the Chief repeated Murray's question: why, when she knew she was down for the night didn't she find a farmhouse and telephone the airport from there? When she answered this question by explaining about the cows and their passion for airplanes, Murray saw the look he dreaded come into the policeman's face, a look of hostile incredulity as hard as steel.

Camilla saw it too and instantly lost her temper.

"All right," she said, with one of those flares of anger that Murray knew so well, "take me and lock me up."

The Chief may have been a little startled but he didn't show it. "What for?" he asked.

"Don't be an idiot. You think I'm lying but you can't possibly think I'd tell lies for fun at a time like this. So you must think I flew my ship in here sometime last night after Pete went home, killed my grandfather for his money and Lucretia Borgia just to make a good job of it, and then flew away again, leaving the tracks on the lawn that I told you about just now because I was afraid you had seen them for yourself. Well, if you think that you ought to lock me up. Have you got your handcuffs with you?"

The motorcycle cop was standing in the doorway, his face wearing the wooden expression of the well-trained subordinate who has just blundered into something interesting that wasn't meant for him.

"What is it, Walsh?" Hopkins asked.

"Mr. Ballard is here with two of his assistants, and the man from the Coroner's office came in the same car. I said I'd tell you they were here."

"I'll be down in a minute," Hopkins told him crisply, and then waited until he had heard the heavy footsteps well on their way down the stairs before he turned back to Camilla. Possibly the interruption had given him a minute or two that he wanted.

"My dear young lady," he said, "I haven't the faintest idea that you've killed anybody but I was surprised for a minute by what you said about the cows. You must forgive me. Apparently it affected your guardian here much the same way. I am going to ask you not to leave the place for the present without my permission. We will inconvenience you as little as possible." With that he nodded and left them. A moment later they heard him greeting the new arrivals in the hall below.

"Sorry I blew up, Pete," Camilla said. "I'm beginning to see why people go and confess things they never did. It makes them stop watching you."

He couldn't think of anything comforting to say but he pulled her up close and let her cling to him for a minute. Presently she steadied her breathing, released herself and turned to face him.

[91]

"All right, Pete," she said. "But I want you to tell me something straight. Do you think Hopkins, if that's his name, is as big a sap as he's pretending to be?"

"I wish you'd talk the English language," said Murray irritably, by way of toning her up. "You can when you like. What I suppose you mean to ask is whether the Chief is really unsuspicious of either of us or is pretending to be in the hope that we'll betray ourselves by trying to cover something up. Is that what you meant by asking how big a sap I thought he was?"

With a little laugh she picked up his hand, rubbed her cheek against it, and then led him to a window-seat, clear of litter, where they could sit down and look out.

"You're an old peach, Pete," she said. "That's the question all right. Now come along with the answer. Only what do you mean by talking about 'us'? He *couldn't* be a big enough sap to suspect you."

"I'm the last person known to have seen your grandfather alive. I was shut up alone with him for the better part of an hour and even by my own story I told him some things he didn't like. Also, he showed me how to work the secret drawer in his desk, and according to the Chief's theory, that's where the pistol was kept. But even so, he's more likely to suspect me of being your accomplice than of being a murderer on my own account.

"The way the experts begin their analyses of these cases is by asking about two things: motive and opportunity. I had a perfectly adequate opportunity. I could have done the whole job, up-stairs and down, in the time I'm known to have been alone with him, and no one in the household saw either of them alive after I left. But when it comes to motive, I'm a great deal of a failure. You see, your grandfather was a valuable client of mine and whatever he might do, within broad limits, it was to my interest to keep him alive as long as possible. But you, on the contrary, had both motive and opportunity."

"Yes, I had a motive, all right," she agreed reflectively. "I'd come home from school, you know, to try to get Lucretia's job and keep her from marrying grandfather. You remember I told you I'd put arsenic in her soup if I had to to keep her from marrying him. You could testify to that, I suppose. I didn't get her job, and I thought she was going to marry him. I almost did, for a fact. Well, so I flew my ship in here early this morning while there was still dew on the grass and let myself into the house . . ."

"How did you do that?" Murray interrupted. "You haven't a key."

"Through the study window where Nelson found the screen pushed up.—Oh, that was locked, wasn't it?"

"Perhaps you locked it yourself after you got in," suggested Murray.

"Yes, of course," she agreed. "Well, then I found my pistol in grandfather's secret drawer. That would have been easy. Grandfather heard me and came down the private staircase and I shot him. And then I went up-stairs and shot Lucretia. And then I came over here into her room to find out whether there were any —well, you know, documents and things—and climbed out this window on to that tin roof and down the water-spout—I've *done* that more than once—and took off and flew around a while and came into the airport and telephoned you."

The coldly reasonable manner she had tried to maintain in the construction of this hypothesis had failed her rather toward the end. "Pete," she gasped in conclusion, "are *you* absolutely sure that that isn't what happened?"

"Absolutely," he told her comfortably. "On cross examination I could tear you to rags. If you came and did it early this morning, how would you account for the fact that both your grandfather and Miss Parsons were dressed in the clothes they were wearing at dinner last night? And when you left your grandfather's room up-stairs to come across the hall into this one, how did you lock the door behind you? There's no spring lock on that door. You have to turn a key and that key is still in its keyhole on the inside. And besides, as a matter of fact, the pistol was not in the secret drawer. Your grandfather didn't keep it there. It wasn't there when he opened the drawer for me and he told me nothing was missing from it."

She drew a long shaky sigh of relief.

"Now we're through with that piece of nonsense," he went on, "I'll tell you what I think about Hopkins. I think he's found out more than he's telling. He probably knew before you told him that you were an aviator and that you'd kept it dark from your grandfather. He probably knew, or guessed at, the sort of relation there was between you and Miss Parsons. He probably found out from some one of the servants that you'd been out all night and that nobody knew where you were. He's probably discovered by observation that I'm weak-minded enough about you to tell any necessary lie to get you out of trouble.

"That adds up, of course, to a total that makes us worth watching; so he's gone rather out of his way to put us off our guard. I think he saw that I recognized your pistol at the first glance and I see now that I made a serious mistake in not acknowledging it. I think he dangled his theory of murder and suicide by Miss Parsons with the idea that we might conceal something or lie about something in the attempt to confirm it. And I think we'll be watched every minute, I just as carefully as you, though perhaps not so obviously. We'll have to live with no more concealments than a couple of show-window demonstrators until they put us out of our misery by finding the real murderer. So what we'll have to do is to make it a rule to answer every question truly, no matter what the admission involves, and without stopping to see what it involves."

"All right, I'll try," she agreed, dully. "But Pete, suppose they never do find him. And suppose circumstantial evidence . . ."

"Circumstantial evidence can't prove an innocent person guilty," he interrupted sharply. "The fingerprints on the pistol, if they find any, won't be your finger-prints, and the tracks outside the study window won't be your tracks."

Camilla had been listening to something else. "What

do you suppose they want of us now?" she asked. "That motor-cop is coming up-stairs again."

She had identified the man correctly and his errand made a startling little coincidence with what Murray had just been saying. The Chief would like to have them come down into the dining-room to have their finger-prints taken.

"Please don't be alarmed or feel insulted," Hopkins said to them as they answered his summons. "This is merely for purposes of comparison."

The finger-printing didn't appear to disturb Camilla. She showed a normal curiosity about the process and its results but nothing more. Murray saw a shade of disappointment go over her face over the absolutely non-committal way in which both sets of prints were studied; she'd probably hoped the expert would say, "Well, you aren't the people we're looking for, at all events."

What really taxed her courage, though, was Hopkins saying to Murray, "Come with me into the study, if Miss Lindstrom will excuse you for a while." She caught her breath preparatory to a plea that she be allowed to come in too, then thought better of it, nodded assent and drifted disconsolately down the hall, through the veranda, and out on to the lawn. From where he sat in the study Murray could see her searching for something; probably to discover whether those airplane tracks still showed. Nobody seemed to be paying any attention to her, but probably some one was.

He couldn't make out what Hopkins wanted of him here in the study. All he'd done so far was to introduce him to Ballard and ask him to sit down, indicating the chair he had sat in last night during his talk with Mr. Lindstrom. Possibly, he thought, their only reason for bringing him in here was to separate him from Camilla.

The body had been removed from the study and the room looked about as it had last night. Murray watched and made what he could of the scraps of conversation he caught between Hopkins, Ballard and the others. They were getting a very slim harvest of finger-prints, both in the study and in the room above; none, in fact, except what proved to be Lindstrom's, Lucretia's, or Murray's own. The significant fact was that on the critical surfaces, the door-knobs, the front of the secret drawer and the stock of the pistol, they found no prints whatever. All had been wiped clean.

This last fact, they all perceived, destroyed the hypothesis that Miss Parsons had shot the old gentleman herself and then committed suicide. If she had shot herself her prints would have been found on the stock of the pistol. If she had shot her employer deliberately she might of course have worn a glove or have wrapped the pistol butt in a handkerchief. And then she might, in a sudden revulsion, have killed herself without discarding this precaution. But in this case the glove would have been on her hand or the handkerchief on the floor. But no glove or handkerchief were to be found.

The experts didn't seem to care whether their discoveries fitted into an intelligible picture or not; for the present all they wanted was facts, all the facts that were discoverable while the scene was fresh. Doubtless they were right about it. But the compulsion upon Murray was to think. For a while the horror of what had happened in this room since he had last sat in this chair made it impossible for him to see anything clearly or to find a beginning from which he could proceed in an orderly way. But presently all at once a puff of wind blew the fog away.

This was literally what happened. The air of the room was so heavy with the acrid smoke of flash powder that at last they had opened the window. The fresh breeze that blew in reminded him of the draught that had caused Mr. Lindstrom to send Lucretia to find this open window. That was the beginning Murray wanted. The chain of events leading to the double murder had somehow or other started then.

Had that window been open all the while they had been sitting at dinner? That was possible, of course, but not very likely. The pushed-up screen which had attracted the chauffeur's daughter's attention this morning could never have escaped Mr. Lindstrom's eye while he sat in that room by the last of the daylight waiting for it to be time for dinner. But it must have been nearly dark out-of-doors when Miss Parsons came in to shut it and she might easily enough have failed to notice that the screen wasn't in place.

All this strongly suggested, though of course it didn't prove, an intruder, such as an ordinary porch-climbing burglar, who had chosen the hour when he knew the family would be at dinner to get into the house in that way. It would have been, Murray thought, a perfectly easy thing for an active man to do, for in addition to the very old Japanese ivy which grew over that part of the wall there was a stone coping which marked the top of the basement.

Lucretia, coming in to shut the window, had locked it as well. This fact, as it happened, was proved by her thumb-print on the latch. But where was the burglar when she closed the window? Well, of course, he might have fled when he heard her coming, getting out the way he had just got in. Or he might, especially if informed about the plan of the house, have already climbed Mr. Lindstrom's private stair to the room above; or he might have hidden himself behind the paneled door at the foot of it.

But none of these alternatives satisfied the known conditions. They failed to account for the length of Miss Parsons' absence from the dining-room and for the change in her manner which Murray had wondered about on her return. Something had happened in the study to detain and excite her and the likeliest thing for it to be was an encounter with the person who had got in the window. If she had found a stranger lurking there in the dark she'd have screamed or fled. It must, then, have been some one she knew, some one she recognized instantly, and some one whose presence was, if not expected, at least easy to account for.

Hopkins might point out that Camilla would fulfil these conditions admirably. Miss Parsons wouldn't cry out at sight of Camilla. She would have paused for a whispered explanation of Camilla's presence there and she might have found the explanation exciting enough to have shown in her manner when she came back. But whatever hour the authorities might choose to assign for Camilla's deadly visit it couldn't possibly have been that hour. Only an hour earlier she had been having her airplane filled with gas at the little home-made landing field a hundred miles away. She couldn't have got back except by airplane in that length of time. She might have landed silently, Murray supposed, with the engine cut off, but no airplane could have taken off again from that lawn during the time that Murray was in the house without a row that would have brought Mr. Lindstrom raging out like a lion. And certainly no airplane had been standing on the lawn at the point where he and Camilla had seen its tracks when he drove Mrs. Smith down to the gate. No, whoever Miss Parsons had found in the study, it wasn't Camilla.

And yet who could it have been if not Camilla? There was no one else in the household whose presence in that room at that hour wouldn't have been unaccountable to Lucretia except on a basis of guilty prearrangement. And how could such a meeting have been pre-arranged? She couldn't have known that her employer would send her to close that window just when he did.

The breeze was freshening again; a strong puff of it now blew in, fluttering the loose papers on the desk and causing Hopkins, who happened to be the only other person in the room at the moment, to glance uncertainly toward the open window. Murray was looking at something else: at a small slip of blue paper that was sliding toward him across the floor. Its shape and color reminded him of something—of something he'd caught a glimpse of last night while Mr. Lindstrom was showing him the mechanism of the secret drawer and stating his suspicion that his secretary had designs on the twenty-five thousand dollars in currency which he kept locked up in the safe. Could that fantastic suspicion of his have pointed to the truth?

"Hopkins," he said, and the timbre of his voice made the policeman jump, "have you looked in that safe?"

"No," the Chief answered. "It's locked and we didn't see the necessity of having it drilled. We tested the combination knob for finger-prints and found nothing."

"No prints at all? Not even Mr. Lindstrom's? And you didn't find his memorandum of the combination in the secret drawer where he told me he kept it?"

The Chief stared at him an instant in silence; then strode to the telephone. "I'll send for a man to open the safe at once," he said.

Murray cautiously picked up the drifting slip of blue

paper from the floor and held it out to him. "I don't believe you'll have to telephone," he remarked. "That just blew out from under something and it looks like the missing combination to me."

Hopkins took it without a word, frowned at it and turned it over. The blank side of it bore a remarkably fine impression of the rubber heel of a man's shoe. "Somebody's stepped on it," Murray said with a grin. "The thing must have been kicking around all the morning."

Hopkins didn't reply to that observation. "You open the safe. I'll call the numbers to you as you go."

Murray obeyed, kneeling before the safe in order to get his eyes near enough to the dial to read the small numerals on it. Presently he moved back and pulled the door open. A glance was almost as much as they needed, for a bunch of keys on a ring dangled from the keyhole in the inner door and the compartment which that door closed upon was empty.

"Thank God!" Murray said. "The money's gone."

Hopkins nodded at him sympathetically. "I feel more or less the same way about it, myself," he said. "I suppose there's no doubt about it. We'll have to go through the contents of the whole safe, though, to make sure."

The revulsion of relief at surmising a story that couldn't possibly include Camilla in any chapter of it had turned Murray a bit faint. "Sit down in that chair and be a witness," Hopkins ordered good-naturedly. "I can do the rest of this job myself." So Murray sat and watched while Hopkins, in white cotton gloves once more, delicately emptied the safe, compartment by compartment, scrutinized every item and put everything back again.

He hadn't found any money. The search for it had been a mere formality, anyhow. There couldn't be any other explanation of the crime than as a plain professional burglary with two incidental murders, one of the victims being the accomplice the criminal had planted in the house. He'd killed her, no doubt, because he was afraid to trust her with her knowledge that he'd killed the old man. And he had left the weapon beside her to give the thing the look of a suicide, just as he'd locked the safe behind him to conceal the theft of the money. Murray swore at himself impatiently for picking flaws in this story. It *was* the story, wasn't it, even though it did leave some queer loop-holes for speculation? Why look a gift horse in the mouth? Why question an explanation that lifted every shadow of suspicion from Camilla?

And yet . . . Why hadn't this thing happened months ago? Lucretia could have admitted her accomplice then as well as now. And why not in the security of the middle of the night rather than during the precarious hour when they sat at dinner right across the hall? Why hadn't she tried to detain them at dinner? Why had the shooting been done with so unlikely a weapon as Camilla's target pistol? . . .

Hopkins had found something. It couldn't be the money after all, could it?

"Here's something," he said to Murray, "that may prove an answer to the inquiries you've been making about Miss Parsons' past. It's an envelope, sealed with wax and the old man's seal, with her name written across the face and the flap as well. Evidently something she'd given him to keep for her. I suppose I'd better open it."

Murray nodded and said—strangely enough—reluctantly, "Yes, I suppose so." It wasn't that he was indifferent or incurious. He was—almost frightened.

Hopkins slit the envelope and pulled out and unfolded its single enclosure. "That's queer," he said with a puzzled stare. "What do you suppose she wanted with another woman's marriage certificate?—

Hold on a minute, though! It's the same name, isn't it, only in French? Lucrèce Pasteur."

"Lucretia Parsons is a rough translation of it, anyhow. Is it a French certificate?"

"No, English. London registrar's office. But what will specially interest you is that the man she married was Eric Lindstrom."

Eric! Eric and Lucretia man and wife!

The sudden perception of a new pattern, trying to swim into focus but as yet not legible, gave Murray a momentary sensation of vertigo. He went out on the lawn, into the fresh air, to tell Camilla about it.

Chapter V

MOSTLY CAMILLA

THIS was Thursday morning. Eric, grandson of the murdered man and probably husband of the murdered woman, was not due to arrive in Chicago till Saturday morning. Pete and Camilla both thought, and Hopkins, after some demur, agreed, that he should be telegraphed to at once, en route. This decision proved easier to arrive at than it was to carry out, since the telegram which had told them so explicitly how he could be communicated with had disappeared.

They searched the study, they even, remembering how strongly the breeze had been blowing in the window while the screen was up, searched the lawn, but all without result—a small mystery that was annoying from its very irrelevance. Murray had had the thing in his hands, of course, and had read it through, but among all its wealth of details he was able to remember nothing but the name of the sleeping-car and that for its absurdity, Carborundum.

This served, however, for when they called up the Pullman Company they were told that this car was traveling eastward with the *Continental Limited* and that it would arrive at Ogden at four that afternoon. The telegram they dispatched to Eric at that point informed him that his grandfather "and his secretary, Lucretia Parsons, or Pasteur" had been murdered. If she was his wife, they reflected, this would convey the news to him.

His reply, which Camilla received late that night, didn't settle the question whether she was his wife or not. He said he was horrified by the double tragedy but he asked that no change be made in any of their arrangements in order to wait for his arrival.

She handed it over to Murray with the remark that Eric couldn't have changed much in eight years, as this was exactly like him. "He'd like to have them both buried and out of the way before he gets here."

"Well, he can't be accommodated in that," Murray said rather grimly, for he agreed with Camilla. "There can't be any serious doubt that he is married, or was, to Lucrèce Pasteur; but the only way of knowing Lucretia Parsons is the same woman is to have him take a look at her. We'll have the funeral Saturday afternoon, as planned."

Murray had packed a bag and come out here to stay with Camilla until Eric should arrive. He made short dashes to his office when need arose, but most of the time he was right here, talking to or fending off reporters, keeping up Camilla's spirits, which was easy except when she got to thinking about Eric, and using his good offices in the war between Hopkins and the Coroner's office.

The ground of disagreement, here, was this: The Coroner, human enough to want all he could get of the publicity surrounding this very sensational case, was anxious to turn the inquest into a full-dress trial, take a lot of testimony, expose all clues, and, as far as possible, "solve the mystery" on the spot.

Hopkins' argument was that the only business of the Coroner's jury was to find the cause and manner of death and that the verdict of wilful murder by person or persons unknown, which was all they could arrive at in any case, could be reached after hearing purely formal evidence from two or three witnesses. And, further, that every bit of unnecessary evidence brought out at the inquest, everything they knew that they superfluously gave away, would make the eventual capture and conviction of the criminal so much more unlikely.

Murray felt that Hopkins was right and sided with him, tactfully at first but applying more pressure, of a frankly political sort, as it became evident that this was necessary. The Coroner gave in, at last, sulkily, and the inquest was held Friday morning in the parlor of the undertaking establishment in Oak Ridge where the bodies were, a mere deputy instead of the great man himself presiding. He may have regretted afterward that he didn't appear in person, for the reporters and sensation seekers got one unexpected plum out of a proceeding that was meant to be purely perfunctory.

The Coroner's physician, Hopkins, Murray, Sophy and Nelson were the principal witnesses and all of them—but Sophy, whose tendency to wander into irrelevances had to be checked—limited themselves to facts which bore on the commission of the crime. But Nelson, happening to remark that it was his little daughter, Ruth, who had called his attention to the raised screen at the study window, and the child being present in the room, the deputy coroner called her to the stand.

She was very demure and so completely self-possessed that the deputy coroner, after patiently explaining the nature of the oath and administering it, paid her a perfectly superfluous compliment; said he was sure she was a very smart little girl and would make an excellent witness. "Now," he said, "don't be frightened but just tell us exactly what happened. You were walking along with your father up the drive from your house to Mr. Lindstrom's . . ."

The little monster instantly corrected him. "Oh, no," she said, "it wasn't like that at all. You see, I gave him a head start and didn't catch up with him until he'd got quite a long way from our house, because there was something I wanted to tell him in private. It was something important about what had happened last night. I don't mean this last night but the night that was last night then. I wanted to tell him after he'd got away from mother, because he and mother had been having a fight—I don't mean hitting; just talking—about whose fault it was that the key of the gate was lost."

The visible consternation of the parents of this prodigious little creature over this statement of hers was enough to convince the deputy coroner that here was something worth going into. He waved them both back into their seats. "If you mean by the 'gate' the iron entrance gates to the Lindstrom place go ahead and tell us what you know about the loss of the key. When was it lost—if you know?"

"Well, all I know," said truthful Ruth, "is what father and mother were talking about at breakfast. But you see, it was like this: father drove Mrs. Smith—

she was the housekeeper at Mr. Lindstrom's house—
to Oak Park to catch the train in Mr. Lindstrom's
big car, because Mr. Mossop—he's the gardener—
hadn't come for her in his car in time. He came ten
minutes after they'd gone and he was sorry he was late
because he'd had a blow-out.

"But when mother went out to lock the gate after
father, she couldn't find the key to lock it with. She
thought father had it in his pocket and had just forgotten to stop and lock the gate behind him. So she
was cross and she stayed up. She turned on a light so it
would shine on the gate and she stayed on the porch and
never took her eyes off it until father came back. She
told Mr. Mossop about it when he came to explain why
he was late, and Mr. Mossop said that was like these
husbands, they were always making trouble, and then
he went away.

"Father was gone quite a long time, but when he
came back and mother started scolding him for having
carried off the key, he said he'd never had the key and
that she'd unlocked the gate for him herself so she must
have put it down somewhere and forgotten what she'd
done with it. She said *he'd* had the key last when he
let Mr. Murray out, and he said yes but he'd hung
it up on the hook in the vestibule where it belonged,

and he'd never seen it nor touched it after that.

"They hunted for the key for a while but they couldn't find it, so then father went and got a chain and a padlock and locked the gate that way for the night. But they were still cross and quarreling about it the next morning. And that's why I wanted to talk to father when he was by himself."

The importance of this bit of testimony was evidently considerable, since it showed that the gates had stood closed but neither locked nor watched for part, if not all, of the time between Murray's departure in his car and Nelson's with Mrs. Smith in the Rolls-Royce. If the murderer had made his escape through this gate he must have done it at this time, while the Nelsons and Mrs. Smith had been sitting in the cottage awaiting the arrival of Mossop.

It was only by luck that the child was not dismissed from the stand at this point in her testimony. Indeed, when one of the jurors rose in his place and asked the little girl what it was that she had wished to talk to her father privately about, the deputy coroner would have dismissed the question as a mere irrelevance if the look in the child's face hadn't arrested him. Her former complacency collapsed at the question, and she said she'd rather not tell. She looked imploringly at her mother but there was no support now in that quarter.

"We put people in jail," the deputy coroner said severely, "when they refuse to answer proper questions."

So the child, sniffling now a little, began again.

"Well, we have supper quite early—half past five—and after supper that night, father and mother said they were going out for a little while and for me to answer the gate bell and not let anybody in that I didn't know, and I asked if they'd bring me some candy from the village, because that's where they were going, and they said yes, if I was good. Well, and when they'd been gone quite a long time, Mr. Murray rang the bell, and I knew him so I let him in and he gave me ten cents for opening the gate for him.

"Then he drove away up to the big house, and I thought probably father and mother would forget about the candy, and I thought it would be better for me anyway if I didn't eat it just before I went to bed—because mother says that's bad for me—so I went across to the barbecue and bought two candy bars. And then after I'd bought them and while I couldn't get across the road because there were so many cars coming, I thought I saw a man go in through the gate. I got across as quick as I could and locked the gate and hung up the key in the vestibule. I wasn't really quite sure that I had seen the man go in. I saw him for just a minute and then he wasn't there when the next opening between the cars came along. I walked around a little while looking for him, and then all at once I thought I saw him looking at me over the top of a bush, and I was frightened and ran back into the house. And the next morning when Sophy came and said she thought something had happened I thought I'd better tell my father about it. But I didn't, because after we found Mr. Lindstrom had been killed anyway, I thought it wasn't necessary."

The involuntary half-laugh which her conclusion evoked slackened the tension more or less and probably helped give the deputy coroner a notion that the second instalment of the child's narrative had been more than half romance. He tried to get her to describe the man but she was so completely blank as to his size, age and coloring—all she was sure of was that he wore a cap and had his hands in his pockets—that another ripple of something like amusement ran over the room.

Neither Camilla nor Murray shared in the general skepticism. As Camilla said afterward, if the child had been inventing this character she'd have been able to describe him, all right. Finally she began to cry and was allowed to get down from the witness chair and run to her mother.

Murray and both the Nelsons were recalled to the stand. The two men fully corroborated her story so far as they severally came into it, and her mother's testimony, when her turn came, contained a real addition to the tale. She would have been a more completely credible witness if she hadn't so obviously felt that her little daughter, forgiven now, had been despised and laughed at.

She remembered now that she had been interrupted while she was getting her supper by a ring at the gate bell, and that going out to answer it she had found a youngish, rather poorly dressed man, with a cap pulled down over his eyes and his hands in his pockets, too, who had wanted to see Mr. Eric Lindstrom, and on being told that Mr. Eric was in California at present, had then asked if he might see old Mr. Lindstrom. She had told him that he couldn't; that Mr. Lindstrom didn't see any one except by appointment, and had gone back to her kitchen, leaving the man still gazing, with a rather unpleasant intentness, through the barred gate. She added that she had had this would-be visitor in mind when she had so carefully instructed her little daughter not to let any one in that she didn't know.

This concluded the testimony. The Coroner summed up, criticizing both the chauffeur and his wife rather severely for negligence, and even implying a criticism upon Murray himself. The jury went out and almost immediately returned, with the only possible verdict, "Wilful murder by person or persons unknown."

As soon as the inquest was over Murray went to town and didn't return to Oak Ridge until just in time for dinner. Camilla, as he perceived the moment he looked at her, had been flying and it had done her good. They dined alone together for the first time, as it happened, since the tragedy. As a matter of fact, it was the first formally served meal at the regular hour since that ghastly dinner on Wednesday night when Murray had dined with old man Lindstrom and Miss Parsons.

Camilla had dressed for it in a summer evening frock and she looked almost disconcertingly grown up to Murray. It was hard to realize she was the child who so recently had been plaguing and cajoling him into letting her have her way about everything under the sun. She had taken without hesitation her old place at the table and Murray, though not without hesitation, had taken Mr. Lindstrom's. He felt, somehow, that it would be better not left vacant. But there was no shadow of the old man's presence over the meal, nor of the presence of Eric Lindstrom's wife, if she had been his wife. The only shadow was that of Eric himself. Murray was planning to get up early the next morning and drive in town to meet his train.

When they left the table Camilla led him out on to the west veranda where she had had them swing a hammock and place a couple of rattan chairs from the conservatory. She held a match for Murray's cigar, lighted a cigarette for herself, nodded him to a chair and stretched out in the hammock, quite comfortably but with more attention to decorum in the matter of the disposition of her skirt than was usual with her. It was one of those new long skirts, which was one reason, perhaps, why she looked so grown up.

"You were right about flying," he remarked. "It both relaxes you and tones you up. You haven't looked as much at home with yourself as this for days."

"I had a good time," she assented. "There was a big cloud with a flat top, about four thousand feet up, that I practised making landings on. Oh, not really, of course. Just pretending.—The way I'm pretending now."

"What are you pretending now?" he asked.

She disposed of her cigarette before she answered that question. "Various things," she said at last. "That this is just a regular evening and not a special one; that nothing's going to happen to-morrow; that it's you who are going to live here—instead of Eric.—It's so *nice* like this. Already. When they've hardly wiped up the blood."

He had nothing to say to this, for the hollow assurance that she was going to like Eric better than she expected was one he couldn't bring his tongue to. She broke the silence a moment later in a way that showed she had roused herself from her day-dream.

"I did something besides have a good time, over at the field this afternoon. I found who made those tracks on the grass that pretty near got me tried for murder. It was just what I thought. One of the student pilots over there took off in a ship very early that morning in too much of a hurry to wait for the engine to be warmed up properly. It began to miss just as he got to the edge of the field, which is when they tell you never to try to turn around and come back, so he set it down in our yard. Then the engine revved up all right and he took off again.

"It was all perfectly correct except that he shouldn't have flown at all at that time because there wasn't any instructor on the field. So he's keeping it dark. He said I might tell Hopkins, though, confidentially, and

I have. The Chief said he wasn't as disappointed about that as he would have been yesterday morning. He must have thought those tracks were a clue of some sort, even if I didn't make them.—And then changed his mind later, at the inquest."

"Do you know," Murray asked, "if he takes the child's story, about the man with a cap and his hands in his pockets, seriously?"

She nodded. "He asked me if I did, when we were driving back from the inquest, and when I said yes, I believed every word of it, he said he was inclined to agree with me. And just before dinner when I came back from the field, I found him playing some sort of game of hide-and-seek with little Ruth among the bushes down by their cottage. He wouldn't be doing *that* for fun so he must have been trying to get something more out of her. I don't see what good it does him, though, if she can't describe the man any better than that."

"It fixes the time of the murder rather precisely," Murray observed. "If you take it in connection with the loss of the key it gives you pretty much the whole sequence. The man slipped through the gate while the child was across the road buying her candy bars. He hid in the bushes until he saw her hang up the key on

[121]

the hook in the vestibule. Then he made his way up here, circled the house to get the geography of it and to see that we were actually at dinner. I don't suppose the shades were drawn. They never are. Then he climbed in the window and Lucretia found him—and for some reason didn't give him away.

"She probably showed him the private stair to Mr. Lindstrom's bedroom. That doesn't make sense but it happened—or something substantially like it. He must have shot them both within a very few minutes of my leaving the house with Mrs. Smith. Anyhow, he followed along to the cottage some time before they had got tired waiting for Mossop. He stole into the vestibule—that would have been a ticklish half-minute for him—unlocked the gate and made the mistake of taking the key with him. He may have meant to lock it after him and then lost his nerve. Any trifle would have been enough for that: somebody over in the filling station looking at him, or a passing car slowing down. He very likely had blood on him and he had twenty-five thousand dollars in currency in his pockets."

Camilla sat erect. "Well, perhaps so," she conceded, "but I don't believe the money was what he came for. Which of them do you think he murdered first, Pete? Grandfather or Lucretia?"

Murray sat up too, under the impact of this question. "The natural assumption was that he killed Mr. Lindstrom first; and then killed her because she knew too much. There are some pretty soft spots in that story, though. How do you tell it?"

"I don't know if I *can* tell it. But look. Do you remember who Mrs. Nelson said the man in the cap asked for? Eric. Well, and he knew Lucretia, too, or she'd have screamed when she found him in the study. If he knew them both he probably knew them together. They may have done something to him, in Europe, somewhere; something treacherous that would make him hate them. Maybe they framed something on him so that he would have to go to prison and they could get married. And when he got out of prison he ran her down."

"That has the makings of a good melodrama," said Murray, "but why, in that case, wasn't the sight of him even more terrifying than that of a strange burglar would have been and why didn't she scream?"

"It isn't as hard as you seem to think," Camilla told him. "Maybe she didn't know that he knew what she and Eric had done to him. Maybe she saw him a second before he saw her and had time to think. Maybe he had something on her that even Eric doesn't know about. If she screamed for help he'd only get out the window again and wait for another chance. But if she pretended to fall for him and hid him up-stairs in her room . . ."

"In *her* room!" Murray broke in.

"Yes, of course. She took him up grandfather's stair and through his room. She had to do that because you'd have heard her if she'd gone the other way. He'd be safe in her room for as long as she wanted to keep him there; till morning, anyhow. Pete, she *must* have taken him there. Who else would have torn her room up, the way it was. He was looking for something— in a hurry. And that's why she was in such a hurry to get back up-stairs.

"I don't know what she meant to do. She may have meant to kid him along and keep him quiet any way she could and then in the middle of the night shoot him and pretend he was a burglar who had just climbed in her window over the porch roof. It doesn't matter what she meant to do, because when she went up-stairs again she found he'd left her room and gone back to grandfather's.

"They were both in there—that's what you think, isn't it?—while you and he were talking in the study. And you heard her scream through the speaking-tube.

Maybe that's when she saw he was on to her and meant to kill her. He might have just found my pistol in grandfather's bureau. She may have told him about the money in the safe in the hope that he'd take that and go. But he shot her, anyway, and then he heard grandfather coming and shot him on the stairs.

"And then everything was quiet and he knew nobody had heard anything—I guess it was lucky for me I was out in the pasture with the cows just then—so he went back and put my pistol beside her so it would look like suicide—only he made a mistake and didn't squeeze her hand against the butt to leave her print on it. Probably he lost his nerve the way he lost it later with the key, at the gate. And then he took the money out of the safe and locked it behind him and shut the study door behind him, which locked itself, and walked out the front door."

The girl drew a long breath, lighted another cigarette with a hand that shook a little and subsided into the hammock. But Murray continued sitting tautly still, leaning forward on his elbows staring at her.

If at the outset he had patronized her story a little, he had dropped this attitude like something hot when she pointed out the inescapable inference that Lucretia had actually conducted the man in the cap to her own bedroom. He'd felt a sort of shudder go over him at the young girl's matter-of-fact surmise that Lucretia had meant to kill him in that room in the middle of the night and then denounce him as a burglar.

At the end of a long silence when she'd finished he said, very seriously, "I've never really believed in feminine intuition until now, but that strikes me as a very fine instance of it. I haven't a doubt that you've told me substantially what happened in this house that night."

" 'Feminine' nothing!" said Camilla. "Pete, have you ever had anybody look at you the way that Chief of Police looked at me? If you'd ever been out all night without an alibi, with what looked like your tracks near the scene of a murder, and your pistol beside the body of a person you'd felt like murdering often enough, it would make *you* think."

"Can you go any further with it?" he asked. "Any further than the gate, I mean."

She answered that she hadn't been able to think anything out beyond that point, but she left the sentence hanging in the air and he waited for her to go on.

"Oh, it isn't reasonable," she burst out at last. "It's nothing but a feeling. I've got a feeling the murderer will come back. If he's got away clean this time—and

I suppose he has because a man with twenty-five thousand dollars in his pocket could hide awfully well—pretty soon, when everything has quieted down, he'll come back and we'll have another murder here, Pete."

"I don't think that *is* reasonable," he said, trying to speak dispassionately. "He's made a good haul and he's satisfied his vengeance. What more can he want than that?"

"He's only satisfied half of it;" she argued, "that is, if he had a grudge against Eric, too. He hasn't done Eric any harm; he's made him rich and he's got him rid of a wife that he must have thought of as a pretty bad mistake. It's plain enough from Eric's telegram that that's how he does think about it. And anyway," she concluded weakly, with a childish shiver, "things like that always go by threes, don't they? And we've only had two. You can call *that* intuition, Pete, if you like."

"I don't like," he told her crossly. "I call it childish nonsense." But as he spoke he seated himself beside her on the edge of the hammock and gathered up her cold little hands between his big warm ones. "It's time you went to bed. I'm going myself because I've got to get up at an ungodly hour and drive in to meet Eric."

Over something between a sob and a laugh she said,

"You may find me here when you come back with him and you may not. I may take my ship and fly off somewhere and never come back. That's what I feel like doing."

He gave utterance to no shocked protest at this idea of hers. Instead, he held her quietly for a while as though considering it seriously and then said, "You can go away if you like. There are plenty of nice people who'd be delighted to take you in for as long as you wanted to stay, around here or in the East, whichever you chose. It's natural that the place should have got on your nerves after all that's happened here."

"It hasn't," she insisted. "I love the place. It isn't ghosts I'm afraid of. And I don't want to go and visit any of your nice sympathetic friends—on the Maine coast or anywhere else. Oh, I'm all right. Don't worry about me. I'll tell you what I would like to do, though. I'd like to come into town and live with you in your apartment. I suppose you'll say that wouldn't do, but I don't see why. It's nothing to what we have done often enough, when we were traveling around together all over the place. Wouldn't you *like* to have me do that?"

He didn't, somehow, feel like joking with her just then so he answered simply, "Yes, I would. But you know as well as I why it wouldn't do. You're—rather suddenly—a grown-up young woman. I've been gloomily aware of that fact all the evening. From now on, the only man you can live with respectably in his apartment will be a man you're married to."

She gave a little laugh which, though still a bit shaky, sounded more like her natural self and said, "That wouldn't worry me. I'd marry you like a shot if you asked me to. We could do that to-morrow morning, instead of you going to meet Eric."

He let go of her rather suddenly and caught his breath. That was one to her. He didn't often let her startle him. But the next moment he said, "I'll tell you what *is* a good idea. Come in and meet Eric with me. That'll be better than waiting here and you'll be all right as soon as you've seen him."

She said in a tone of impatient concession that she supposed she should. Then she blew her nose in a loud and unsentimental manner and got up from the hammock. "That really is a good idea, Pete," she then said. "I'll tell Sophy coffee at six. That sounds like getting ready to fight a duel, doesn't it? And I've a hunch that that's what it ought to sound like.—Come along. Let's lock up and turn in."

They saw to the doors and windows and put out the

down-stairs lights in silence. But when they were about to part at her bedroom door she caught him suddenly in a tight embrace and clung to him. She wasn't crying but her voice was so muffled against his chest that it was hard to make out what she was saying.

"I've always loved you, Pete; ever since I was a wretched little scared kid eleven years old.—Even if I have made you a lot of trouble.—I've never cared a damn about any one else. You won't chuck me now, will you?—Because I'm grown up? And turn me over to Eric?"

He said, "I won't chuck you for anybody; not if you live to be a hundred." Then, feeling curiously shy about it, he kissed her good night and walked away toward his own room.

She wasn't feeling shy, though, for she called after him with perfectly reestablished composure, "You'd better come and pull me out of bed about ten minutes to six unless I'm up by that time."

"All right," he agreed.

Murray was a long time getting to sleep, that night. He heard the big clock down-stairs strike every hour and every half, till half past two.

Chapter VI

AFTER EIGHT YEARS

It took more than Sophy's coffee to make Prentiss Murray feel like anything human at half past six in the morning after a night like that. He bitterly reproached Camilla, whom he hadn't had to pull out of bed, for looking so damned bright-eyed. On the drive in town, though, he was glad he had her along, for instead of talking to him she snuggled down within his arm with her head on his chest (they were in the big car with Nelson at the wheel) and calmly finished out her night's sleep that way. She had done that scores of times in the past when they had toured together and it was, somehow, reassuring—after last evening's ambiguities.

They got in a little too early and during a dismal chilly wait of nearly half an hour in the station concourse the girl's mood of nervous apprehension came back upon her. She wandered away from Murray and then retreated to him because she thought some people had stared at her. She dragged him with her to see if there were any later news on the train bulletin.

Finally, just as the locomotive was appearing down at the far end of the train shed she clutched his hand and asked, "Pete, do you suppose we'll even know him?"

"I expect to," he said coolly. "Oh, and so will you. Don't be silly. It's possible, though, that he won't know you. You've changed a lot more since you were eleven years old than he will have since that time."

"He's seen my picture," she reminded him. "Remember the one I had taken two or three Christmases ago? I sent one to him, in one of my sentimental fits about a long lost brother, and a soppy letter. He answered with a rotten little French compliment on my looks as if all I'd sent it for was to be admired. I tell you, I don't *like* him, Pete! I never have and I . . ."

She had continued to cling to his hand as they walked down the platform and at this point, with a sudden squeeze, he silenced her. They were opposite the steps of a car with Carborundum painted on the side of it. The porter was busy handing out the bags to the red caps and on two of them, a gladstone and a kit bag, Pete and Camilla saw the initials "E. L." He was really here, then.

They gazed intently at the first two or three passengers to alight. Could this be he? No, not possibly. Nor this. When he did appear they both gasped, he was so astonishingly the same Eric they both remembered. He saw Camilla first and his eyes widened at the sight of her; then he smiled, strode across the rampart of bags that lay between them, pulled her up by the shoulders and kissed one cheek, held her off for a better look, and then drew her back and kissed the other.

"And we were wondering," said Camilla with a break of laughter in her voice, "whether we'd know you or not."

Eric let her go to shake hands with Murray, saying as he did so, "Well, it's nice to know I'm still recognizable. But it's terrible that you should be here. My God, at what an hour you must have got up! I think it must be sheer waste of money, telegraphing people not to meet one at the train."

"A good deal has happened," Murray reminded him rather shortly, "since that telegram was received at Oak Ridge."

"Yes, of course," Eric agreed.

He hung his head as he spoke and looked embarrassed; and this was characteristic, too, Murray remembered. So, for the sake of saying something the older man remarked, "The whole telegram struck your grandfather as an unwarranted extravagance. He was deeply concerned about it. It was the last thing he talked to me about."

"Yes, it would take him like that." Eric laughed as he spoke and then proceeded to explain: "I was amused at his being so mistaken. There was, as I suppose you will have guessed, the best of reasons for that telegram."

Murray hadn't guessed but he didn't feel like asking at just that moment. He inquired instead if Eric had had breakfast and on learning that he had not, suggested that they stop for it in the station restaurant. "I'm hungry myself," he admitted, "and I suspect that Camilla, here, is famished."

Her only response was a nod and as Eric didn't seem to care much for the idea, Murray went on. "It will save time, and that's a consideration this morning."

"Oh, very well," Eric agreed, dismissing his objection, whatever it had been.

Facing Camilla across the breakfast table her newly restored brother took a frankly pleased survey of her and presently said to Murray, "Isn't she marvelous, our little Camilla? At least you can not blame me if I marvel.—Because you were, my darling, at eleven an absolute little brat. That photograph you sent me—

was it two years ago?—I simply disbelieved. Without the memory of it I shouldn't have recognized you at all. And yet to-day it falls as far short of doing you justice as I believed it went beyond when I received it."

Camilla, Murray saw, was getting ready to explode. It always annoyed and embarrassed her to have people insist on dwelling upon her looks, even people she liked. She said, speaking low and looking off across the room, "I don't feel so very much changed since I was eleven. My feelings are about the same, anyhow."

Murray intervened hastily. "I wonder if you'd mind telling us what *was* your reason for sending that first telegram. I suspected a reason in it when your grandfather gave it to me to read but I wasn't able to figure it out."

"Well, but naturally!" said Eric. "The person it was meant to inform was poor Lucretia. And to give her a chance, if she wished, to communicate with me before I arrived. She never would be given a look at a letter of mine. The old gentleman would be sure to bury it in some hole, like a squirrel." He laughed at the thought and expanded it a little. "He always did remind me of a squirrel—an old gray slightly motheaten squirrel, tucking things away."

It was a rather apt description and one that had

amused Murray the first time he'd heard Eric strike it off, ten years ago, perhaps. But it didn't amuse him this morning, nor did it amuse Camilla.

He looked from one of their faces to the other and then said, "If you good people are expecting that I shall exhibit a broken heart either over my grandfather's death or over that of my unfortunate wife, you are going to be disappointed. For one of them I never felt any affection, and for the other, I soon lost what I had. I suspect, my dear Camilla, that our feelings toward both of them are remarkably alike. Why then should we keep up a pretense between ourselves?"

She flushed deeply but didn't attempt to answer the question.

Murray intervened again. "You do know then that the woman who was murdered in your grandfather's house actually was your wife? From your second telegram we weren't perfectly sure."

"Well, I know," said Eric, trying to state the exact degree of his knowledge accurately, "that my wife has been living at my grandfather's house and acting as his secretary. I have even heard from her directly. That's sufficient, isn't it?"

"Sufficient for us," Murray told him, "but not for the Coroner's office. One of our reasons for meeting the train, our only reason now for hurrying your breakfast, is to get you out to Oak Ridge as early as possible to view the body and formally identify it so that a burial permit can be issued. Feeling as you do about her the ordeal won't be as severe a one for you as we feared it would be."

"Surely that can't be necessary," the young man protested; "nor even very helpful, judging from the gruesome accounts I've been reading in the papers as I came along. Is she even—recognizable?"

"I had no difficulty recognizing her," Murray told him, shortly. "If she was Lucrèce Pasteur she was your wife, and that's a question you'll have to settle for us. I'm afraid we'll have to insist upon it. And since there's quite a lot to do getting ready for your grandfather's funeral this afternoon the less time we waste the better."

"I meant to make it plain in my telegram, that I didn't want you to delay the funeral for me."

"It wasn't done for you," said Murray, and that closed the conversation. Their breakfast was put upon the table just about then and they ate it in almost unbroken silence. Toward the end Eric showed signs of getting over his sulks but not, as it proved, because he had surrendered to their wishes.

"Since you have committed me to a formal funeral," he said as they were about to leave the restaurant, "you must give me a chance to equip myself with something that is fit to wear. Excuse me for an hour and I will follow you to Oak Ridge dressed in accordance with the proprieties."

"An hour won't do you any good at this time in the morning," Murray pointed out to him. "It's only eight o'clock and the shops won't be open till nine. But if you'll go out with us now you can go through the necessary formalities in a very few minutes and then Nelson can drive you back and you can buy all the clothes you like."

Eric shrugged and laughed. "You win!" he said, throwing an arm around Camilla and starting toward the door with her. "It is simply no use, my trying to have my own way. They will never let me have it."

Well, that was Eric all over, of course. As self-centered and spoiled a young man as ever lived he went through life under the delusion that it was just one frustration after another. There was, though, or had been, a sort of factitious charm about him. It had been more attractive at twenty than at thirty, Murray reflected. Perhaps that was why it didn't work better with Camilla.

They didn't talk much, driving out in the car. Eric said a few of the things about the appearance of the Northwest Side that an artistic young man who had spent the past few years traveling about Europe would say, but not in an offensively superior manner. As they drew near the village of Oak Ridge Murray suggested to Camilla that she drop him and Eric at the undertaker's and drive on home, sending the car back for them as soon as she got there, but she squeezed his hand in sharp dissent and said, "I'm going wherever you go, Pete."

She hadn't reckoned with the possibilities of a busy Saturday morning on Main Street. The curbs were solidly parked with automobiles and even the sidewalks were crowded with people in idle dilatory motion. Around the doors of the undertaking parlor they were crowded too thick to move at all. Their car was recognized, of course, and this made matters worse. Nelson got as near the doorway as he could and stopped; out in the middle of the street, necessarily since he couldn't get to the curb. Murray got out quickly, noticed that the street was in a horrible mess from having recently been oiled, and said, "Better change your mind, Camilla. This is no place for you."

She would probably have done so if it hadn't then

appeared that Eric had not understood that the bodies were here and not at the house, and had no intention of getting out at all. Their car was blocking all traffic in the street and the crowd was getting worse every minute. Eric, looking out the other window, seemed preoccupied with something else and it was not until she took him by the arm and actually started dragging him out that he roused himself to follow her. She was feeling pretty well shaken by the time they got inside and was glad to be offered a stuffy little cell of a "parlor" to sit down in and be by herself. Hopkins and the deputy coroner had been waiting for them; as she withdrew she saw Murray introducing Eric to them.

As soon as he could Murray followed her into the little reception-room and sat down beside her. Neither of them tried to say anything; this was neither the time nor the place to go into their real feelings about Eric.

Presently Hopkins, too, came in and sat down with them. They'd learned to like him in the last few days and to feel a great deal of confidence in him. "I sent Mr. Lindstrom into the morgue by himself," he explained. "Her appearance will be a good deal of a shock to him, I expect, and it's easier to take a thing like that if there's no one watching to see how you take it." He turned to Camilla. "It must have been quite an ordeal for you this morning, meeting a long lost brother who was so near a stranger to you. Did he look natural?"

"Not only looked, but acted," said Camilla. "You'd think a person would change a little in eight years. But almost everything he said and did made me think how exactly like him that was." Murray confirmed this with a nod.

Eric was looking pretty white when he emerged a few minutes later from the morgue. He said simply, "Yes, it is she," and signed without scrutiny the paper that was waiting for him on the desk in the undertaker's office. But as soon as this was done he made it plain that the principal thing on his mind was the procuring of proper clothes to wear at his grandfather's funeral. He wanted Nelson to drive him straight back to town without a preliminary visit, even of the briefest, to the home he hadn't seen for so many years. "I shall see it soon enough," he explained. "And as you know, I've no sentimental longings connected with it."

His going straight back to town would leave Camilla and Pete without transportation, but Hopkins met this difficulty by offering them his car, with a policeman chauffeur to bring it back, so for once at least Eric was allowed to have his own way without amendment.

They dismissed the Chief's car at the gate and walked the rest of the way, up the long shaded road to the house, glad of a chance to stretch their legs. As they came in sight of the stiff old-fashioned mansion they paused.

"I hope Eric goes right on hating this," Camilla said. "Because if he does, he won't want to stay here long.—Pete, don't quarrel with him about grandfather's money, however much of it he wants for his share. Give it to him and let him go back to Europe." That was the only thing she had to say about Eric.

She might have liked him better if she had not driven in town with Pete and had had her first meeting with her brother when he arrived at the house clad in his newly purchased clothes. There was—as there had always been—a touch of the actor about Eric. Now, in black morning coat and derby hat, he abandoned the manner of cold flippancy that Camilla and Murray had found so offensive at breakfast.

His arrival found them on the porch and he paused to chat with them there while Nelson and Sophy were carrying his bags up to his room. He seemed thoughtful and looked rather pale in his black clothes. "The place has changed," he said. "I don't know exactly how, but it looks—mellower than I remember it." He went up alone to his room and didn't come down again till they were summoned to lunch.

This was a hasty and distracted meal, served in the breakfast alcove. The funeral had been set for three o'clock and already the undertaker's men were rattling down their rows of little folding chairs in the two drawing-rooms and the dining-room.

As soon as she could leave the table Camilla went up to her room to lie down for a while and then to dress once more in the black frock she had worn for her grandmother's funeral so few months ago. Murray was going to be busy; two of his women friends from town were coming out, he had told her, to help with the arrangement of the flowers. Camilla knew them but to-day she didn't want to see any friends of Pete's and have them sympathizing over her. As for Eric, he could take care of himself; it was his own house, wasn't it?—at least as much his as hers. So she locked her door and didn't come down until the sound of cars in the drive told her that people were beginning to come.

It had been arranged by somebody that she and Pete and Eric were to sit by themselves in the study where

[143]

they could see the minister and hear him read the service. They had put the room to that use at her grandmother's funeral but the choice of it to-day seemed rather gruesome. She found the two men already there and sat down beside Pete.

Eric's look of thoughtful gravity which had descended upon him, apparently, when he put on his black clothes was deeper now than ever. Through the whole service—and it included a long, stupidly eulogistic sermon that made Camilla fidgety—he hardly moved.

A surprising lot of people had come to the funeral: bank directors, of course, and people like that; trustees of hospitals and charities; church people; and about half the village of Oak Ridge, partly to show the real respect they felt for their old neighbor and partly from a lively curiosity to see, if possible, the spot where he'd been murdered. Of the crowd that packed the house there was hardly a handful of people that either of the two young mourners in the study knew.

For this reason it had been arranged that they should sit here quietly by themselves until the congregation had been dismissed. Then alone, the three of them, in the big car, followed the hearse, the pall-bearers and the minister to the cemetery.

Until all this was over Eric's half-entranced manner

[144]

never lifted. He responded appropriately when he was spoken to, allowed himself to be guided here and there, greeted some among the pall-bearers when his attention was called to the fact that they expected to be remembered, but on his own initiative he did nothing. No wonder he shrank from funerals, Murray thought, if they took him as hard as this. But when, on their return from the grave, they stood alone once more in the hall of the swept and garnished house, he said, with a sudden air of coming to life, "I'm going to get out of these infernal clothes. You change too, Camilla. We don't have to go on looking black any longer."

She was quicker about it than he and she was sitting with Murray in a couple of deck-chairs in the shade of the house on the east lawn when Eric emerged in search of them. He had gone out of mourning with a vengeance; he was in golf knickers, cap and sweater, and a pair of brand new and extraordinarily brilliant sports shoes. He seemed to have changed his mood, too, just as completely.

"Do you know, I'm falling in love with this place," he proclaimed excitedly. "It's got a real charm about it. And the trees are bigger than they used to be, I'll swear they are."

Murray pointed out, a little dryly, that trees had a

way of getting bigger if you let them alone long enough. As for Camilla, she said nothing at all.

Eric came over to her, holding out a hand as if inviting her to be pulled up out of her chair. "Come along," he said. "Take me for a tour of the grounds. I want to see it all—gardens and everything—while the light is exactly like this."

Camilla, hiding her reluctance and dismay as well as she could, accepted her brother's hand and got to her feet. But she turned immediately to her guardian and held out her hand to him. "Come along, Pete," she said.

The peremptory way in which she had included him in the party embarrassed Murray a little. It seemed perfectly natural that Eric should want to take his sister off by himself, and so far to-day he hadn't been alone with her for an instant. He might easily come to consider Camilla's guardian as a meddlesome nuisance if he had to be dragged into everything. But for the present apparently nothing was further from Eric's thoughts. He seconded Camilla's invitation with a smile and an outstretched hand of his own.

Murray indignantly rejected both these offers of assistance. His age was not yet so advanced, he said, that he required to be pulled up out of a chair.

He felt a friendlier disposition toward the young heir at that moment than he had felt before, and though he comprehended Camilla's dismay over Eric's announcement that he was falling in love with the place, he believed that if that emotion were genuine it might go a long way toward curing his ward's curiously deep dislike of her brother.

They started off on their tour arm in arm; that is to say, Eric had taken Camilla's arm while she clung to Murray. There was a way you always went when you showed people the grounds: around through the shrubbery, past a little ornamental pond and along a carefully cut out vista to the big grape arbor which formed the entrance to the flower gardens.

But the walk to-day was interrupted before they got as far as that. They happened not to be talking and their soft-shod feet made no noise over the close-cropped meticulously combed lawn, and coming out of the concealment afforded by a dense copse of hazel bushes, they surprised little Ruth, the chauffeur's daughter, at her curious game of hide and seek. This time she seemed to be playing it by herself without the assistance of Hopkins, the Chief of Police.

She was startled and embarrassed, as a child of that age so often is by the fear that he has been caught making himself ridiculous. But this moment had passed and she was rapidly recovering her characteristic self-assurance, when she got her first good look at Eric, he having been the last to emerge from behind the bushes. At him for an instant she stared in sheer stupefied amazement, her mouth hanging open and her eyes so wide that they appeared to be sticking right out of her head. Then she turned and ran in the direction of the chauffeur's cottage, which was about a hundred yards away, crying, "Mamma! Mamma!" in terrified accents as she fled.

The three of them stood staring after her in silent astonishment until the sound of a door flung open and slammed shut told them that she had reached her haven.

"What in the world," said Eric, "do you suppose has got into that child? It was me she screamed at. She lives here on the place, I suppose? Do you know if the sight of strangers usually takes her like that?"

"Quite the contrary," said Murray. "She's usually . . ."

He glanced around at Eric and broke off short. Camilla was staring too, and under the impact of the same surmise. For Eric's hands were plunged deep in his pockets and his cap, for shade against the low sun, was pulled well forward over his eyes!

Murray pulled himself together after the break and went on speaking. "The child's got a wild idea of some sort in her head. Shall we go on to the garden?"

"No," Eric said decisively. "I'm curious to find out what that wild idea was. That was Nelson's cottage she ran for, wasn't it? Is she his daughter? Let's follow and find out what sort of story she's been telling her mother."

He didn't wait for them to agree to his proposal but started off through the shrubbery in the direction of the cottage by the gate. They followed, dubiously, and overtook him just as he knocked on the door.

"When a child screams at sight of you and flees for her life," he observed while they waited for it to be opened, "you naturally want to know what sort of spectre she thought it was she saw."

It was Nelson himself who, after a little delay, opened the door for them, and they could see by his flustered manner that he was very much upset. He was alone in the room he admitted them to, a large pleasant sitting-room. The kitchen was behind and through the open door into it they could hear the suppressed whimpering of a child's voice and now and then a woman's, in a low tone, admonishing or comforting her.

"I suppose you've come about my little girl, sir," Nelson said to Eric after he had insisted that they all sit down. "I'm sorry if she's been foolish and made a scene. I hope you'll overlook it, sir. You see, with the murder and all, and she naturally excitable, it's been too much for her."

Eric said, in a friendly and entirely reassuring way, "I'm not surprised that it has been too much for her. I'm only sorry that I should have frightened her. But I'm curious to know why. What sort of monster did she think I was?"

Nelson didn't want to tell and it took pressure to get it out of him.

"Why, you see, sir," he explained at last, "the evening before your grandfather was murdered she thought she saw a man looking at her over the top of a bush—a man with a cap on. It gave her a bad scare, sir, and she's thought ever since that the man she saw was the murderer. It seems she was playing detective just now—that's all she does, these days—and she saw you, with your cap on, sir, looking over the top of a bush and it gave her a start. I hope you'll excuse her being so foolish about it."

All this was audible in the kitchen, of course, and at this point it brought the child's mother upon the scene. Perhaps she thought her little daughter's folly was being unduly dwelt upon. The room was half dark by then. She saw Camilla first and spoke to her. Then, as her husband said, "This is my wife, Mr. Lindstrom," and Eric stood up and came forward to shake hands with her, she got her first good look at him.

She was staring into his face so hard she didn't notice the outstretched hand. "If you are Mr. Eric Lindstrom," she said, "you can't be the man who spoke to me at the gate last Wednesday evening. But you look enough like him to be his twin brother." She went on staring in the tense silence for a moment more. "Liker than any twin I ever saw," she added then, and went back into the kitchen.

CHAPTER VII

HOPKINS MAKES A SUGGESTION

THERE was a period of a few long seconds after Mrs. Nelson's withdrawal to the kitchen during which none of the four who were left in the room spoke, moved, or even, it may be believed, drew breath. Then Nelson, probably at that moment the most single-minded of them, since he felt his job hanging by a thread and didn't mean the thread to be broken if he could help it, got himself together sufficiently to cross the room and shut the kitchen door upon his wife. That done, he turned and said very earnestly to Eric, "I hope you won't be angry, sir. She's been through a great deal since the night of the murder, and she never can bear to have our little girl's word doubted or made light of. But she didn't mean that the way it sounded. She'll apologize to you, sir, as soon as she comes around."

"But, good God!" cried Eric. "What for? She doesn't owe me any apology. If the man who spoke to her at the gate Wednesday night looked as much like me as . . ."

He broke off so sharply there that Camilla looked around at him. She hadn't felt that it was possible to look at him before. He had begun speaking as naturally as a man just emerging from such a shock as he must have received could be expected to. But now that he had fallen so suddenly silent he appeared to Camilla like a man in a daze, as if some sudden surmise had overwhelmed him.

The next instant, though, he pulled himself out of it, with a characteristic shake of his head, and turned to Murray, saying, "I beg your pardon. It is probable that she thinks of it differently: not as a resemblance but as an identity. She thinks I *am* the man who was here last Wednesday evening." He paused to swing a quick look into Camilla's face, and then back to Murray's. "For that matter," he went on, his voice sharpening a little in timbre, "you two may be considering that as a possibility yourselves."

"I suppose we might have considered it," said Murray, "if it hadn't been for the telegram you sent us from the train at Ogden."

Eric pulled in a long breath and let it out with a rush. "I'd forgotten that telegram for the moment," he said. Then turning back to Nelson he went on, "I think your wife may have given us a real clue which will enable us to find the murderer. Thank her for me, will you, for being brave enough to tell us so frankly what was in her mind. And tell your little girl she needn't be afraid of me any more." By way of finally assuring Nelson that he was not offended he shook hands with him, and then with Camilla and Murray, left the cottage and started back toward the big house.

Their tour of the grounds was abandoned without discussion. Eric said, after they had walked a little way in thoughtful silence, "Your friend the Chief of Police—is his name Hopkins?—should be informed of this, I think, without a moment's delay. If he can come out here before dinner and talk to me I think I may be able to tell him something that will interest him."

It had struck Murray, too, that Hopkins ought to be told, and it relieved him of a slight embarrassment to have the suggestion come from Eric. Accordingly, as soon as they reached the house he went into the study to call up the Chief.

Coming back to rejoin them in the drawing-room a few moments later he found Camilla alone. "Eric's gone up-stairs to dress again," she explained, "—for dinner, this time. It seems his trunks have just come.

I told him I wasn't going to dress and that I knew you weren't, but that didn't make any difference. He said he'd be happier that way. Is Mr. Hopkins coming?"

"As quickly as a side-car will get him here. I didn't tell him anything over the phone, of course, except that we had some new developments."

Camilla led him out on to the south porch where they could watch for Hopkins' arrival, and the two of them sat down on the top step and lighted cigarettes. Of her own accord and in a mood of comfortable meditation, Camilla began talking about Eric.

"He seemed nicer this last half-hour than I thought he could be," she said. "You know, it's a sort of test of what you really are to come out of a shock, like being practically identified as your grandfather's and your wife's murderer, and still be fair and decent to everybody. It's in the first gasp of a surprise, before you've had time to think, that you give yourself away. He was really sweet about it. It's funny how important his clothes are to him, though. I don't remember his being as fussy as that, do you?"

"I remember him as rather dandified," Murray answered, "but not as carrying it to such lengths as this. We may be wronging him, though, darling. It may have been pure tact that made him give the excuse of wanting to dress so that we might have a chance to tell Hopkins anything that was on our minds without him around to cramp our style. It's worked out that way at least, for here comes Hopkins now."

Their peaceful cozy appearance seemed to surprise the Chief. "I brought Walsh along," he remarked, "not knowing whether we were going to have to shoot our way into the house to rescue Miss Camilla, or what. Apparently a gun play isn't going to be called for."

"No," said Camilla, "all we need is a little conversation. Why don't you let Walsh go back, and stay and have dinner with us? Eric wants to talk with you and he's up-stairs now dressing for the occasion."

Plainly Hopkins was pleased by the invitation but he thought a minute before accepting it. Then saying he'd like that very much he sent the motor-cop back to the station in his side-car and vaulted informally to a seat on the brick pier that little Ruth had once occupied on the occasion of a talk with them.

Murray glanced back into the empty hall and then said crisply, "Here's what we called you about. Eric has just given Mrs. Nelson and that child of hers the shock of their lives. The child saw him with his cap on looking at her over the top of a bush and ran home screaming, under the belief that he was the man she'd seen here in the grounds Wednesday night. Well, you might think her mother's later identification of him as the man who had talked to her at the gate was simply by way of backing her daughter up. But you wouldn't think that if you'd seen her. She as good as said she didn't believe a resemblance could be as strong as that, implying, of course, that she thinks Eric *did* drop in here that night for the purpose of committing the murders."

The tense silence in which Hopkins listened to what Murray was telling him and the frozen immobility of his body showed how the news had surprised him and what he thought of its importance. He asked, a little while after Murray had finished, "How did young Mr. Lindstrom take all this?"

"As well as a man could take a blow like that. He didn't blink the possibility that Camilla and I might suspect him. It was his own suggestion that you be informed at once. He showed perfectly frank relief when I pointed out to him that the telegram he had sent us from Ogden Thursday afternoon proved that he couldn't have been in this house at ten o'clock the night before." He hesitated a moment and then went on. "I suppose it *doesn't* prove that, really."

"No," Hopkins agreed, "by itself it doesn't prove a thing. He could have had an accomplice on the train for no other purpose than to send that telegram in answer to one of yours that he could have foreseen. But as it happens I can provide him with a better alibi than that. I had a couple of my men meet that train this morning. They questioned the Pullman conductor and the porter, dining-room steward, barber, and so on. Those crews make the whole trip with the train, you know."

"Then there *were* people staring at us while we waited on the platform this morning," Camilla broke in. "Pete, here, thought it was all my eye."

"I'm sorry their work was so coarse," Hopkins said with a grin, "but they were there all right. Oh, I may as well make a clean breast of it. I never believed you'd murdered anybody, Miss Camilla. But I did think when I saw those airplane tracks on the lawn and found how impressed everybody was with the telegram that told so very definitely what train and car and section young Mr. Lindstrom was traveling east on, that these two facts might belong together. I knew you were a flyer—I'd heard about that before the murder—and I knew you were more or less keeping it dark. So it struck me that Eric might have dropped in unexpectedly that night, quarreled with his grandfather and murdered him, and had got you to fly him out west somewhere to give him a start toward meeting the train he was supposed to be on.

"When I found that his wife had been killed at the same time as his grandfather I was surer of it than ever. His telegram shook me but I explained that as the work of an accomplice. So I was ready for action this morning and I was from Central Missouri regarding that alibi of his. But I was wrong. I had a good theory but it just wasn't so. There isn't the slightest shadow of a doubt that Eric Lindstrom got on that train Wednesday morning in Los Angeles and that he was on it at the moment his grandfather and his wife were being murdered."

"It must strike you as a rather queer coincidence, though," Murray observed, "that the man who probably did commit the murders happened to look as much like him as that."

"Well, yes," Hopkins agreed; "though it may not seem so strange when we find the man. Identifications are the most untrustworthy sort of evidence in the world. That of the child in this case amounts to very little. She can't have had much of a look at him either time she saw him. Remember how completely she

[159]

failed to produce any sort of description of him on the stand, yesterday. She'd probably have run screaming from any strange man in a cap whom she saw looking at her over the top of a bush.

"Her mother's has more weight, of course, and I've no doubt she's entirely honest about it. All the same, she's a very impressionable, highly emotionalized woman. Given half a chance, she'll see what she's expecting to see, every time. Her thinking that Mr. Lindstrom was too like the man she talked with at the gate to have been any one else gives us a good general idea of the appearance of the man we're looking for, but that's about all it does."

"That doesn't make it seem very hopeful that you'll ever catch him," Camilla said, discontentedly.

"I hope to catch him," Hopkins assured her. "There may be surer ways of tracing him than by his looks. There's one I want to ask you about," he went on, turning to Murray. "Has it occurred to you that though old Mr. Lindstrom was willing to run the risk of being robbed by keeping twenty-five thousand dollars in currency in his safe, he would have tried to lessen the risk by keeping a memorandum of the numbers of the bills—keeping it not in the safe, of course, but somewhere else—so that he'd have a chance to recover them if they were taken?"

Murray couldn't see why he hadn't thought of that himself. It would be so exactly like the old gentleman that it wasn't possible to believe he hadn't done it. It would be like looking for a needle in a haystack, though, to try to find a small memorandum like that among his endless files. For sixty years he had never destroyed anything; not even, Murray believed, a receipted bill or a notice of a directors' meeting. All the same, the job would be worth attempting seriously and systematically.

Camilla laughed indulgently and patted his knee. "How will you start?" she asked. "Begin back at eighteen-seventy-two and work your way down through? I'll bet I can find it quite easily and without being systematic at all." She jumped up without giving him a chance to offer her a bet that she couldn't and said she was going in to tell them to set a place for Mr. Hopkins. She was gone rather longer than this errand would have taken. Indeed, Eric came out before she did, in the fourth costume they had seen him wear that day.

Camilla, it appeared, had changed too into the dress she'd worn the night before, or one a good deal like it, Murray couldn't be sure which. Its character was the same, anyhow, and she disconcerted him once more by looking grown-up in it. Dinner was announced just as she joined them and they trooped into the dining-room, Eric recalling that he was the host in time to drop back at the dining-room door and insist that the others precede him.

Camilla seated herself to-night at the foot of the table and motioned Hopkins and Murray to the places on her right and left hand. Then Eric, a little reluctantly Camilla thought, took his grandfather's old chair at the head. The strangeness of seeing him there struck all of them silent for a minute; then Camilla said to Hopkins, "I'm glad you stayed to-night. It's nice not to have any vacant places."

"I'm glad, too," Eric put in. "I suppose you've told him what happened down at Nelson's cottage this afternoon, and I take it he wouldn't be sitting down to dinner with me if he was planning to arrest me as the murderer and lock me up in the village Bastile."

The joke struck Murray as being in rather poor taste, but Hopkins took it pretty well.

"Not on the evidence that's appeared so far," he said with a smile. "In fact I'm a little surprised that Mrs. Nelson's outburst seems to have impressed all three of you the way it did. It's exactly as broad as it is long, of course. That is to say, it completely cancels itself."

He turned toward Camilla as he spoke. She answered him with a puzzled look and said, "I suppose the others see what you mean but I don't, even now."

"Why, it's like this," Hopkins answered. "The man she thought she identified Mr. Lindstrom with was the man she talked to at the gate. Now assume for a minute what we know to be impossible, that Mr. Eric Lindstrom *was* here on Wednesday night, having previously prepared an apparent alibi that he was on a train traveling this way from California. Assume that he meant to kill his wife and his grandfather and then escape to the west and get on that train in time to make his alibi good; assume that he did steal into the grounds at a moment when the gate was standing open and unwatched by little Ruth, who'd gone across the road to get her candy bars.

"So far you have a perfectly consistent, carefully planned, skilfully executed crime. There's just one piece of evidence that completely contradicts and demolishes it. And that is Mrs. Nelson's testimony before the Coroner that the man she now thinks is Mr. Lindstrom rang the gate bell about six o'clock that evening and asked to see Mr. Eric Lindstrom—in other words, himself—or failing him, his grandfather. The essential feature of the plan we're assuming him to have taken such trouble to carry out was that he shouldn't be seen or recognized by any one at all; that it should be confidently believed that he was not here but somewhere else. Yet the only possible purpose he served by ringing the bell and asking for himself would have been to give whoever might answer his ring a chance for a good leisurely look at him.

"So, I say, it's unthinkable. It cancels itself. The man little Ruth saw might have been Mr. Lindstrom here, but the man her mother saw must have been some one else; some one, I should say, who looked a good deal like him—perhaps strikingly like him—but who was demonstrably another man altogether." He turned back to Eric. "Isn't that the way you work it out?" he asked.

Eric nodded. "I don't know whether I could have worked it out that way if I'd been a pure outsider, or even as much an outsider as Pete and Camilla, here. But I'm not an outsider at all. I not only know that I wasn't here that night to ring the gate bell and ask for myself, but I think I've got a pretty good guess who the man was. It broke over me like a wave just about a minute after Nelson's wife turned her back on me and flounced out of the room. I was paralyzed at first, but when I came out of it I thought fast. I told Camilla and Pete at the time that I had a story to tell you that I thought you'd be interested in. Well, this is it. I don't altogether enjoy telling it even now, because it shows me up for such a giddy young ass.

"It was three years ago, just a little more than three years ago. I've learned a great deal one way or another since then." He broke off to light a cigarette and drew in a deep breath of the smoke before he went on. "It began one night in Paris in a crowded Métro train when I found myself staring into a face so much like my own that I was startled. He was a man of about my own height and I should guess of about my age. It was evident that he was as much struck by the resemblance as I was. After we'd gazed at each other a few minutes in silent astonishment, being a young ass at the time as I admit, I spoke to him, idly and jokingly you know, and he answered in the same vein.

"We were talking in French, of course. He spoke it pretty well but with a distinct foreign accent, which is about the way I speak it myself. So presently I tried him in English, thinking that that might be his native language too. He answered, sticking to French, that he understood English a little but couldn't talk it beyond a phrase or two. So then I asked him what his nationality was and he told me he was a Norwegian.

"There was no reason, of course, for my being surprised at that, but I was, and I confided to him that I was a Norwegian myself, or half a one, my grandmother and grandfather having come from there. I added that I'd never visited the country and didn't speak a word of the language. He remarked that this was a pity, since it was a wonderful country and a beautiful language, too. I said I doubted if I ever learned the language but that I was planning to visit the country very soon.

"By that time the train was slowing down for the Étoile, which was where I was getting off since my apartment was in that quarter. He was getting out there, too, it seemed, and we strolled out of the station together. I got a little better look at him then—at his general appearance, I mean. His clothes were neat enough but rather shabby, and his walk had something indolent and indecisive about it; the walk of a man who hasn't really anywhere to go. He was a pleasant attractive chap and I felt a little sorry for him. So, being still a young person without good sense, I suggested that we stop at a café near by and have a bock together. And I went on, since he hesitated a little over accepting my invitation, and added that my name was Lindstrom.

"He jumped when he heard the name and then laughed, rather embarrassed. It was ridiculous, he said, but his name was Lindstrom, too, Emil Lindstrom. I felt uneasy for a minute—it was a real warning, of course,—but he made absolutely nothing of it, dismissed it merely as a rather absurd coincidence.

"What he did go back to when we had begun sipping our beer was what I had said about planning a visit to Norway. Had I been serious? I said I was perfectly serious, that I had only that day visited a steamship office to inquire about the tour to Hammerfest to see the midnight sun. He seemed a little let down by my saying that. It was well enough for mere gabbling tourists, but the country was worthy of something better than that from a serious traveler, and especially from one who had its blood in his veins. He talked a little about it; what one might see if one got out of the tourist rut. It would be a little more difficult but nothing to be afraid of. Of course, to get the real flavor of it one should have the language.

"He didn't go any further with that and neither did I just then. We ordered a couple of cognacs with benedictine for a night-cap.

"Our resemblance fascinated me more and more and by now I had thought out a theory to account for it. We were, no doubt, cousins; fourth, fifth, sixth, the degree didn't matter. Somewhere in the past century we had a common ancestor and both of us had happened to reproduce him. In the interest of discovering who this ancestor might have been I told him grandfather's name and the town he had come from. But he threw cold water on my researches; he took no interest in his ancestors, he said.

"We were on the point of parting without having gone further than that—and I wish to heaven we had. I hadn't drunk enough not to know that it was the sensible thing to do. If he'd made any kind of proposal I should certainly have declined it. But just because he made none and because he had insisted upon paying for one round of our drinks out of a pitifully thin pocketbook, and because, as I have confessed, I was a young ass, I proposed that if he had no other employment that would forbid, he make the trip to Norway with me, as courier. We didn't settle the matter on the spot but we did in a day or two. We spent the rest of the summer touring Norway together."

"You sent me some post-cards," Camilla put in. "One I especially remember . . ."

"Wait, I'll tell you," Eric interrupted with a laugh. "It was the one of the goat under a tree grazing on the roof of a cottage."

[168]

She nodded that he was right.

"Emil made an admirable traveling companion," he went on. "He came as near as any man could to making good his promise that he would show me everything interesting in Norway. And we had good times together—silly, if you like, but amusing. One of our amusements was to mystify people with our resemblance. For we did look enough alike to be mistaken for each other very easily, and the one common language we possessed we talked about alike. The fact that each of us possessed a language which the other couldn't speak at all, or practically not at all, made it all the more entertaining."

"It was true, then," Hopkins asked, "that he spoke no English?"

"At that time I think it was true. Later, when we went back to Paris together, he must have picked up quite a bit of English. He was always at me to try to teach it to him. It was his idea to come back to America with me. It's the idea of every down-and-out European these days to come to America if he can get a chance. But I never could take the time nor the trouble."

"Your relation with him didn't end, then, with the Norway excursion?" Murray remarked.

With an uneasy flush and a hanging head Eric admitted that it had not ended there. "That's where my real folly begins," he said. "He was much easier to take on than he was to get rid of. He was well-bred and he seemed intelligent. But there was simply no way in which he could earn a living, unless by acting as courier to parties going to Norway, and people don't travel to Norway in winter. So I kept him on for several months, until early the next spring in fact, as a sort of valet. It was amusing, and once or twice it was convenient when some idiot escapade of mine might have got me into hot water. Well, I came to realize at last that he was utterly untrustworthy, and I dismissed him."

"Was it a quarrel?" Hopkins asked.

Eric considered. "No, I shouldn't call it that. Why do you ask?"

"I was thinking," said the Chief, "of those escapades you spoke of and wondering whether he left you with a grudge."

"A grudge that lasted him all these years," Eric supplemented with a smile, "and that brought him here to our gate last Wednesday afternoon seeking revenge? No, it certainly wasn't as serious as that. It annoyed him to lose a soft job, and especially since, as I said, he had hoped to come back to America with me. But I think that was all."

"You were planning a return to America about that time?"

Eric laughed. "Oh, I was always planning a return to America. And equally, for one reason or another, I was always changing my plan and putting it off."

Camilla glanced at Pete Murray and saw, she was sure, the same thought in his mind that was in her own. According to the marriage certificate they had found in the safe it must have been at just about this time that Eric and Lucretia had been married. That had been, of course, the reason for this change of plan. But had it been the reason for something else?

"Eric," she asked impulsively, "had Lucretia anything to do with it? With your finding out that he wasn't trustworthy, I mean, and dismissing him?— Eric! Please don't mind. I didn't mean to pry. I only thought if Emil was very angry with her, over something she had done—or he thought she had done— to lose him his job, well, that that might have been the—grudge, you know, that brought him to our gate; looking for revenge not on you but on her."

The sheer consternation which had kept the girl floundering on into deeper and deeper water was fully accounted for by the scowl of undisguised anger with which her brother had greeted her mention of his wife's name. Her apology didn't placate him a bit, either. If he didn't cut her short it was only because he was, for the moment, speechless.

He spoke now, stammering a little in cold fury. "We will not, if you please, discuss my wife. Couldn't you have seen for yourselves that the subject is painful to me? I identified her body for you this morning and she is now buried. So far as I know she had nothing to do with the affair of my discharged valet. Leave it at that."

There was a long moment of intensely embarrassed silence. Dinner was finished and they were smoking over their coffee, so there was no reason for their not leaving the table except that to make a move at that time would have underscored the incident still more unpleasantly. It was Hopkins who came to the rescue.

"I think the whole question of motive may be left aside for the present," he said. "My first job, as I see it, is to find this discharged valet. If his name really is Emil Lindstrom and if he recently came to this country with a proper passport, the immigration bureau may give us a line on him. It would help, though," he went on, turning to Eric and getting out a note-book and a pencil as he spoke, "if you could give me a few additional facts about him. Did you find out, during your summer in Norway together, whether he was actually a distant cousin, and if so what town or parish he was born in?"

"No, I didn't," Eric answered shortly. Now that the heat of his anger had gone by he had fallen into one of his characteristic sulks—his way of acknowledging, perhaps, that he'd been behaving badly. "I don't make it a practise to pry into people's affairs when they've let me see that they want them let alone. I think I've already told you all I know about him. Later, if anything more occurs to me I'll tell you." He pushed back his chair and rose. "I've had about enough for one day, since seven o'clock this morning," he went on. "If you will excuse me,"—this with an ironic bow to Camilla whom he evidently hadn't yet forgiven—"I'll retire."

The others had risen, too, but without waiting for any further move from them he walked out of the dining-room and they heard him going up-stairs.

"You're perfectly right," Pete said to Camilla. "It's amazing that in eight years he should have changed so little. Everything he does is exactly like him."

Hopkins remarked good-humoredly that it had been

an instructive evening, anyhow. Then he thanked Camilla for having asked him to dinner and said he thought he'd better be going back. He turned into the study to telephone for his car but as he was on the point of picking up the instrument the bell rang. "I'll take this since I'm right here," he said to Pete and Camilla. "Come in a minute, though. I've thought of something."

The telephone caller, whoever he was, wanted to speak to Mr. Eric Lindstrom. "Mr. Lindstrom's retired for the night, I think," Hopkins said. "Can't you leave a message?" They both saw a rather intent look come into the Chief's face as he listened to the response to this suggestion. "Just a minute," he said then. "Mr. Gordon Taylor, is that right?" Then he covered the receiver with his hand and said to Camilla, "He says it's personal and he seems a little pressing. Shall we ring for Sophy and have her go up and tell him?"

"I'll go," Camilla volunteered, and darted out of the room. They heard her going up the stairs two at a time. Eric's rooms were on the third floor but two flights meant nothing to Camilla.

"What I thought of," said Hopkins, still keeping the transmitter covered, "was that there might be some information to be found here. Did old Mr. Lindstrom have any sort of genealogical record of the town he came from and who his Norwegian ancestors were? If he did we might at least be able to settle the question whether there was a cousin Emil or not."

"Do you suppose the valet's name really was Lindstrom?" said Murray. "I doubt it strongly myself. It seemed so clear to me that the whole thing was a put-up job—that encounter in the Métro, I mean. He probably got on Eric's trail when he went to the steamship office to find out about trips to Norway and followed him until he got a chance to make the meeting seem accidental—and on Eric's initiative."

Hopkins nodded agreement to this. "Still," he pointed out, "his name may have been Lindstrom. He couldn't have traveled to Norway and back to France without a passport and he'd hardly have chanced calling himself that if his passport read in another name. It might have been forged, of course."

"I don't know of any record . . ." Murray began. "Wait a minute, though!" He had just recalled to his mind the picture of the family Bible reposing in solitary majesty on a little stand of its own in the back drawing-room. He went to get it and was returning with it as Camilla descended the stairs, more slowly and thoughtfully than she had gone up.

"Eric won't come," she said to Hopkins. "He says Mr. Taylor is to leave his number and he'll call him up in the morning." She must have been deeply pre-occupied or she'd have asked Pete what on earth he was doing with that Bible.

Hopkins delivered the message and hung up, looking pretty thoughtful himself: "Mr. Taylor says he'll call again to-morrow morning," he explained. Then he called the police station to tell them to send Walsh for him.

"There are some records in here," Murray said, producing the great volume that was under his arm as the Chief turned away from the telephone. "I didn't stop to try to figure them out."

Hopkins studied the pages of crabbed handwriting in faded ink for a while in silence. "It will take quite a bit of figuring, I expect," he said at last. "If you don't mind I'll carry it off with me."

"Here's something else for you to take along with you," said Camilla. She handed him a small pocket memorandum book bound in dark red polished morocco. Murray remembered it so well that he started at the sight of it. "It was in the drawer where we put all the things that were taken out of grandfather's pockets," she explained. "I stopped in and got it just now. All the last pages in it are full of numbers. Do you suppose they're the bills that were stolen from the safe?"

A glance satisfied both men that she was right. Pete shook his head glumly. "How much was that bet we didn't make?" he asked. "I'd rather you named the figure while we've got Hopkins here as a witness."

But Camilla didn't triumph over him as she might have been expected to do. She said soberly that the bet didn't count and, still grave, accompanied the men out into the veranda.

They could hear Walsh in the side-car coming up the drive. Hopkins, still looking rather preoccupied, said, with the air of a man coming to a decision, "Do you mind my making a suggestion—a purely domestic suggestion, Miss Camilla?"

"No," she assured him, "of course not."

"I think what this household needs just now is a butler—a good competent butler, or houseman, whichever you choose to call him."

Whether she had fully taken his meaning or not Murray couldn't be sure. She said, uncertainly, "Of course we are short-handed, with Mrs. Smith gone, especially now that Eric's come back. I was going to look for some one Monday."

"Well, I can take that job off your hands," the Chief told her cheerfully. "I know just the man for you. And he can report the first thing to-morrow morning, which is just one day better than Monday."

The girl saw what he meant now, all right, but she answered steadily, "That's very good of you. We'll be glad to see him."

"He'll do his work satisfactorily," Hopkins told her. "You needn't be afraid. Only I think it will be better if no one but you two knows that I provided him." He added as they nodded assent to this, "Don't let it worry either of you," wished them a cheerful good night and drove off with Walsh.

Camilla didn't stir till after she'd watched them around the curve of the drive. Then she slumped down on the top step and when Murray seated himself beside her she caught at his hand and clung to it.

"It's true, Pete," she said. "What we were guessing about last night—only then we didn't know who the man was. You know who I mean; the man Eric and Lucretia had done something to. He came and killed her for it but he didn't get Eric. Well, he's come back for him now. He was the man on the telephone to-night."

"Darling, you can't jump to conclusions like that,"

[178]

Pete protested. "It's perfectly wild. Why should a prospective murderer telephone for an appointment?"

He could have ridiculed her fears more wholeheartedly, though, but for that thoughtful look he'd seen in Hopkins' face and for that sudden determination of his to plant a policeman in the house. It was this, of course, that had upset Camilla.—But it seemed it wasn't.

"Listen, Pete," she said. "You know when I went up-stairs to call him to the telephone? I wanted to go because I wanted to tell him I was sorry I'd been so thoughtless, and wouldn't be any more. Well, I knocked on his door and he didn't answer. He has two rooms up there, of course, beside his bathroom and that old closet he used to use for a dark room. I thought he might not have heard so I tried the door. It was locked. But he had heard me, all right, because the instant I turned the knob he called out, 'Who's that?'

"I said it was me and that I'd come to tell him he was wanted on the phone. He opened the door with a jerk—he was still cross, you see—and asked why the devil he should be disturbed for the telephone at this time of night. I said the man wouldn't leave a message and that his name was Gordon Taylor.

"Pete, his face didn't change a bit; but his eyes did. Something happened to them. It was like—like some sort of animal in a corner. He tried to speak so that I wouldn't know. He said, 'Oh, Taylor! He must be a chap I picked up on the train.' And I said, 'Shall I tell him to leave his number and you'll call to-morrow?' and he said, 'Yes, do that.' But his lips were shaking so that he could hardly talk. I watched them: I couldn't look anywhere else.

"Oh, I'll try not to be silly. But Pete, promise you won't go away. Promise you'll stay right here, even if Mr. Hopkins does send a policeman. Something more is going to happen in this house, Pete. It isn't over yet."

He promised readily enough that he wouldn't go away, and then, since it wasn't properly bedtime yet, he played backgammon with her for an hour in the study. It seemed to serve as a perfectly good distraction for she gave her mind to it sufficiently to win a dollar and eighty cents from him before they'd finished.

But a few minutes later, after they had seen to the doors and put out the lights, and as he was leaving her at her bedroom door, she said, "I'm glad your room is right next to mine. Will you mind if I leave the door open a little way after you've gone to bed?"

Chapter VIII

UP IN THE AIR

THIS was no outburst of sentimental rhetoric on Camilla's part. She meant it. And after she'd knocked to ascertain that he was ready to have the door open she came over to his bedside and kissed him good night again, a forlorn little wraith in the faint light that followed her in from her bedroom, despite the gaudy pajamas which, when properly illuminated, showed orange and black in modernistic zigzags.

Every nerve fiber in Pete's body registered a protest against the confusion she created in his mind by being a child one moment, a woman the next, then a child again. There was no such thing as meeting these shifts of hers with the appropriate emotion. He might almost have said, "Get in here and cuddle up with me, since you're so cold and scared," yet he felt himself blushing hotly down to the neck over having thought of such a thing.

He came to the idiotic resolution to sleep very lightly, if he slept at all; nothing deeper than a mere doze, so that he'd be certain to hear if anything happened during the night that could alarm her. The result was that he lay broad awake for three hours or so, though he hadn't had a decent night's sleep since last Tuesday, and then went under as though somebody had chloroformed him.

The next thing he knew the big clock down-stairs was booming out eight, the light of a brilliant August Sunday morning was shining in his face, and the door between his room and Camilla's was shut. It occurred to him uneasily to wonder whether he'd been snoring so loud that Camilla had had to shut it in order to sleep. He didn't know whether he habitually snored or not; he hadn't any way of finding out. If he did, Camilla, confound her, probably knew by now.

He might have gone back to sleep if the roar of an airplane overhead hadn't made him think of her again. He could understand by now why old Mr. Lindstrom had hated the damned things. He wasn't at liberty to hate them himself, not as long as Camilla loved them so. That might have been Camilla herself, whizzing around over the chimney tops with the specific intention of waking him up.

He crawled out of bed and stood at the open window, yawning and blinking at the hard blue sky, looking for her, though he really knew better than to expect that he'd be able to recognize her and have her flutter her handkerchief at him like a young lady out paddling in a canoe. He was somewhat startled, therefore, when her clear young voice hailed him from the ground. She'd gone out on the lawn, it appeared, to survey the sky for herself.

"Did that idiot wake you up, darling?" she called. "It's a shame. But now you are out of bed get dressed and come down and we'll have breakfast together."

Half an hour later when he went looking for her he found her still on the lawn. She was dressed in a sports shirt and blue denim trousers but she didn't look like a boy—any more than the trousers looked like overalls. She kissed him rather absent-mindedly and approved of his necktie and the smell of his shaving soap. He said something about its being a rather decent morning.

"Yes, it's a pretty good day," she assented professionally, "though the air'll get rough later unless a steady breeze blows up."

There wasn't, he reflected, a single thought in her mind but of getting into that damned airplane of hers and sailing around among the clouds. That was why she had dressed this way, no doubt: for convenience in buckling a parachute between her legs. What were women coming to, anyhow! Still wanting men around for watch-dogs when they were frightened but going their own sweet way at all other times without a thought for anybody!

"Did you see anything of Eric down-stairs?" she asked, taking his hand and leading him toward the house. On his shaking his head and grunting out a negative she quickened their pace a little, saying, "Let's hurry up and have our breakfast by ourselves. There's no telling when he'll be down."

He was still deep in his reflections on the unsatisfactory transitional status of the modern woman and though he assented to her plan it was without enthusiasm. She brought him into focus by asking very sympathetically, "Did you have another bad night, Pete?"

He looked around to see if she were grinning to herself, but she wasn't—at least, not externally. "I slept all right after I got off," he said. Then he asked the question that was on his mind. "How did our door get shut?"

"I shut it when I got up to dress, about an hour ago," she told him. That was all right, then, he reflected; but as he glanced around at her he saw she was smiling a little and presently she added:

[184]

"I was going to make you get up then, too, and I looked in; but you were sleeping so nicely and looked so innocent that I hadn't the heart."

He had probably been looking like hell, he concluded, with his mouth open and his head hanging out of bed. He didn't pursue the subject.

Indeed he couldn't have done so if he had wished to for just now as they were approaching the veranda steps little Ruth, the chauffeur's child, hove into view running toward them as hard as she could and panting when she stopped before them like Sheridan's ride. There was no fear in her face, however, nothing but self-importance, and the pants were pure scenery. The child could run like a deer for miles.

"Mother wants to know," the message ran, "whether a man who's come in a taxicab from the village and says he's the new butler is to be allowed to drive in. She said nobody had told *her* anything about a new butler though maybe some one had told father and he forgot to mention it because that would be exactly like him."

"No," said Camilla, "I was the one who forgot. It's all right. We're expecting him. Run back to the gate as fast as you can and let him in."

The child executed a demi-volte and galloped away.

"I haven't much sympathy with chauffeurs as a class," Murray remarked, "but I do hope that there's a compensation in store somewhere, in this life or another, for Nelson."

Camilla laughed shortly but she was thinking about something else. "It's lucky he isn't a real butler or he might have been annoyed at having to wait so long and gone looking for another job. Pete, now that grandfather's dead, couldn't we have some sort of private telephone put in between the house here and the cottage?"

"Do you mean to say there isn't any?" Murray demanded. "Is this what happens every time a stranger appears at the gate? And how did the old gentleman call for his car when he wanted it? Send Mrs. Smith or Sophy down afoot?"

"Well, of course there are hardly any strangers at the gate who are supposed to be let in," said Camilla. "And there is an electric bell that grandfather used to ring: once for Nelson himself and twice for his car. And now I ring three times for mine. Nelson has a telephone of his own so we *can* get him that way— only it's a party line with about fifteen people on it and likely to be busy. And grandfather wouldn't allow them to call us on the phone. They have to send Ruth or come themselves. Of course they hate it and it is awfully inconvenient."

Pete said they'd attend to having a private phone put in to-morrow and went on to reflect aloud upon the fact that a man might be a real villain and yet be better liked than a perfectly honest well-meaning man who indulged himself in petty tyrannies like this. Camilla agreed but with her mind on something else. She must hurry into the kitchen and prepare their minds for the new butler or he'd get there before she did.

Indeed, promptness appeared to be one of the outstanding characteristics of this new functionary. They hadn't been five minutes at the breakfast table before he had relieved Sophy of the duty of serving them, white jacketed and as much at home in the job as if he'd held it for a month. He looked serious and rather young, answered to the name of Carl and spoke with a rather strong Scandinavian accent of some sort. Both Camilla and Pete had for the moment forgotten that he was anything other than just what he appeared to be when he asked a question that reminded them. Would Mr. Lindstrom wish his breakfast served in his room?

Camilla, not knowing how to answer, referred the

question to Pete. He guessed what was in her mind. It might be something of a shock to her brother to have a strange man come knocking at his bedroom door, but, after all, what of it?

"Better go up and ask him," he decided; and after the man had left the room he explained to Camilla, "Eric's lived long enough in France to have got into the habit of having his breakfast served that way; and the airplanes must have waked him long ago."

He had made a conscious effort to speak without venom about airplanes but he hadn't, apparently, been entirely successful. Something in his tone, at least, had caught Camilla's ear but she didn't laugh nor make a face at him as she might have been expected to do. Instead, she finished her cup of coffee rather deliberately and sat back in her chair.

He perceived without being told that they had reached a moment he had been on the lookout for for weeks, ever since she had made her first solo flight. She was going to ask him to let her take him up with her. He had rehearsed his reply to this invitation until he should have known its phrases by heart. He might be clay in her hands up to a certain point but beyond that point he was adamant. A small open-cockpit airplane with her at the stick was, simply, beyond his limit. All her arguments, her cajoleries, her derision, her shameless pettings and snugglings, would be as unavailing as they would be if practised on an old walrus. She'd better reserve them for the effecting of some purpose that was within her powers.

For its background, though, this speech required that Camilla should be sitting on the arm of his chair, rubbing her cheek against his, nuzzling at him like a pony, twisting his hair, laughing at him, scolding him, imploring him not to be a heavy parent. She was doing none of these things now. She was sitting very still in her own chair and not even looking at him—looking out the window. Her face was grave and its naturally high color had receded, leaving it rather pale. When he saw she was about to speak he experienced a panicky wish for reenforcements; for the presence of some one else in the room, even the new butler.

What she said was, "I don't want you to hate airplanes, Pete."

"I don't," he told her, but the disavowal must have sounded as weak to her as it did to him, for she ignored it.

"Grandfather hated them, of course," she went on. "All he knew about them was that they were noisy and that he couldn't keep them from flying over his house.

He was afraid they would fall or that they would drop things overboard on him. I suppose it's natural to feel that way if you never think of them—except from the ground."

He might have pointed out to her that he had flown in an airplane. He had been with her on the occasion of the first flight she had ever made, the one from Berlin to Amsterdam, and by virtue of this experience his point of view must be distinguished from old Mr. Lindstrom's. But this, he knew, she would regard as a quibble. She had told him often enough that those big cabin ships were different; they didn't give you the same feeling. He didn't want to quibble with Camilla while her face wore that tense serious look.

He perceived now as the silence spun itself out into seconds that she wasn't going to ask him to go up with her in her little plane, let alone press or coax him to do so. And in a sort of breath-taking revelation he understood why. She wasn't regarding him across this breakfast table as an elderly guardian to be wheedled into giving her something she wanted, but as a companion, as an equal—that was the compliment she was paying him—with whom she wanted to share an experience that had a profound significance for her.

A sense of having just had a narrow escape, though

from what he didn't stop to explain to himself, stiffened his lips and dried his throat, but as soon as he thought he could command his voice he said, "I'd like to learn to think about them as you do, Camilla—as nearly as a passenger can. When will you take me up with you?"

Even then, though the light and the color came back into her face, she didn't tell him he was an old darling and perch on the arm of his chair to reward him with pats and endearments. She said, "This morning, Pete? Now? It's turning out a lovely day with this nice little east wind to smooth out the air."

She was still serious and a little remote, a new Camilla to his experience, and he was a little afraid of her. He didn't make any of the jokes of the sort that usually arose between them on occasions when he was putting himself into her hands for one purpose or another. He merely said that now was as good a time as he could think of, and walked with her down the hall, catching up his cap from the table as he went by.

Her little car was waiting in the circle—she must have rung Nelson's bell three times before they sat down to breakfast—and without another word they got in and drove off. Mrs. Nelson opened the gate for them—what was she looking so damned benevolent about? he wondered—and they were really on their way. It wasn't five minutes to the main entrance to the field.

Pete realized that there were a lot of things he wanted to think about, but a sort of luminous mist seemed to have settled over his mind that prevented his thinking properly about anything at all. The thing that conspicuously wasn't in his mind, except negatively on account of its remarkable absence, was his approaching flight in Camilla's airplane. He was feeling scared— at least he was experiencing the symptoms of fright, shortness of breath, racing pulse, and a sensation of extreme hollowness beneath his midriff—but this had nothing to do with the flight. It was something else altogether.

Camilla continued remote. She had driven the car with none of her usual *élan,* though she had kept both hands on the wheel the whole time and her gaze straight out ahead. When they left the car and walked out on the field she pointed out a little green airplane that had its engine running and said with satisfaction that that was it and that they were warming it up as she had asked them to. Even when they stood beside it all she said was, "It's a good little ship, Pete."

She spoke with deep feeling but she didn't pat its sleek sides nor talk to it as if it were alive; in fact she proceeded to inspect it in a spirit of cold criticism. She didn't call on him for any raptures, either.

He would have agreed with her that it was little. Its next neighbor in the line was an enormous Ford that was slowly making up its first complement of passengers for a thirty-minute ride as a uniformed attendant sold tickets. Beside it Camilla's plane looked like a Christmas toy. But a dusty-looking man in a khaki coverall who had come out to assist in her inspection seemed to be taking it as seriously as she did.

She held a short technical conversation with him which finished by her deciding upon a change in the scheme of things. "I want Mr. Murray in the rear cockpit, Bill. You get a better view of the ground from there. Do you mind changing the stick so that I can fly it from the front?"

At his nod she took Pete by the arm and led him away. "He can do it while we're getting into our chutes and helmets. Here's Brownie. He'll show you how to put yours on."

This episode of the parachute was unpleasant, apart from its gruesome suggestiveness. The harness seemed insanely complicated and was vilely uncomfortable. It took Brown (he was the pilot who had been Camilla's first instructor) about ten minutes to get him hooked into it and when the job was finished he felt like a trussed fowl.

Brown explained its operation, too, with what Pete felt to be misplaced humor. "It's perfectly simple," he said, walking alongside as Pete waddled out on to the field and squeezed his way through the early crowd of curious spectators. "If Miss Lindstrom tells you to jump, break loose your safety belt, climb out of the cockpit and drop over the side. Count six and then give this handle a yank. That's all. The 'chute 'll take care of you after that."

When Murray rejoined Camilla at the side of the airplane he asked if he mightn't be excused from wearing the contraption. "I'll be a lot more comfortable and just as safe. Because if anything happened I shouldn't be able to use it. I shouldn't have the nerve to jump."

"Yes, you would," said Camilla, smiling a little but still gravely. "Because I couldn't leave the ship before you did. I'm in command and I'd have to be the last man to bail out."

After that he did exactly what she told him to, putting his feet on the places she indicated and settling himself with his parachute under him in the little bucket seat of the after cockpit. When she had him safely buckled in and had made him unfasten the belt a time or two to satisfy herself that he knew how to do it, he said, "I suppose this is to keep me from falling out when you do loops and things."

"There'll be no stunts on this trip, Pete," she assured him. "No loops nor spins nor anything like that. You see, I've sort of got all my eggs in one basket.—And no basket of eggs," she went on with the first gleam of her real humor that he'd seen since breakfast, "was ever carried any more carefully than you're going to be."

Brown, who had been standing by, now took a look over the field. Some idiot from the sidelines, a stoutish roughly dressed man old enough to know better, had wandered out on to the field with the evident intention of walking straight across it. Brown shouted at him to come back but the chap didn't or wouldn't hear, for he kept straight on going toward the eastern border of the field.

"While you're being careful," the pilot said to Camilla, "you may as well take care that you don't kill that damned fool over there."

"The way I'm going to take off," she answered, "he couldn't get in front of me if he tried."

He saw what she meant when she started, for instead of taking off, as she might have done safely enough from her place in the line, she taxied past the hangar to the extreme west boundary of the field where she had a run that would suffice for getting anything with wings into the air. Pete didn't appreciate this, of course, and he had forgotten that the back-breaking angle at which he sat would be corrected as soon as the tail came up and they left the ground, but not even in the extremity of his discomfort did he call himself a fool for having launched himself on the adventure.

Camilla swung the plane around, looked back, not at him but professionally, at the sky over her right shoulder and then over her left, the roar of the engine, loud enough before, doubled in intensity, the seat suddenly became comfortable as he found himself riding level with her, the ground fell away, they were across the river, above the Lindstrom house, and with the realization that their flight had fairly begun the tension of his muscles relaxed.

She kept him up, as he discovered later, for over an hour and she gave him, by climbing to an altitude of well over a mile, his first look at the area bounded by a single horizon in which he had lived practically the whole of his life. The crystalline visibility of everything, thanks to its being Sunday and to the fact that there was an east wind, made it, or should have made it, a really fine adventure in sightseeing. But this aspect of it was somewhat wasted on Murray this morning, for what his mind was looking at most of the time was Camilla.

All he could actually see of her, sitting low in the front cockpit, was her small head snugly encased in a canvas helmet. Once in a while she would turn to shout something at him, or to point out something he was to look at, but in the main he was impressed by her extreme immobility. None of the motions she made in guiding the plane were visible to him. But that helmeted head meant Camilla and served as the focal point of his thoughts.

In this phase, certainly, she couldn't be thought of as a child. Brown's attitude toward her and that of the mechanic she had called Bill would have made that plain to anybody. There was nothing indulgent or patronizing about their manners. She was admitted to their freemasonry on her merits.

Well, was she really a child at all, in any of her relations to life, or had he merely been clinging to the delusion that she was because he couldn't bear to give it up? From the first it had been to him one of the most delicate and charming, as well as one of the most powerful and humanizing influences in his life. He had known of course that it couldn't last for ever. He had even, in jaundiced moments, conjured up future scenes in which she came to him and told him she was engaged to marry somebody who lived in South America, or something equally devastating. But it had always been a much larger and more regal-looking Camilla who had told him these things and she had been telling them to quite an old man, rather bent, perhaps, and very gray.

Sentimental idiocy that was, of course. The future was already here. How long had it been here? How long had Camilla known it was here? How long had she been trying to show him that the old relation between them was nothing but an empty shell, and that, unless an empty brightly colored shell, to be put on a what-not and admired as a souvenir, were to be enough for them they would have to begin something new— and perhaps more hazardous?

Anyhow, he knew now what his narrow escape of this morning had been. By laughing at this serious wish of hers, by failing to see what that wish really was, he could have mummified himself into a cherished relic of her childhood without ever knowing he had done it. Well, he hadn't done it. She had told him just now that he was her whole basket of eggs, and in a manner that showed it to be true—so far.

She had saved up, it appeared, the finest sensation she meant to give him for the last. She throttled down her engine when she was, perhaps, half a mile above the field and glided down to it in three broad turns of a great spiral. Murray dismissed his philosophizing for a complete surrender to the thrill of what felt more like flying than anything they had previously done that morning. It surprised him, therefore, to find when at last they were on the ground again that Camilla was bitterly dissatisfied with her landing. Technically— that is to say from Brown's point of view—she didn't regard it as worthy of her skill.

He couldn't hear exactly what she said, having caught above the noise of the engine only the words "rotten" and "tail high," but he made out that she was asking if he'd mind if she took off once more, just for the sake of landing properly. He nodded a ready enough assent, she did the equivalent of stepping on the gas— "giving it the gun," he believed the phrase was—and once more they raced across the field, and were above the Lindstrom place at not much more than the altitude of some of the higher buildings in the loop whose windows he sometimes looked down to the street from.

Even in his rear cockpit, from which the view of the ground was supposed to be better, he couldn't see what was immediately below them, but he saw Camilla visibly start and look down, and the next instant, with the sensation that his eyes had somehow lost their moorings and a disconcertingly empty feeling inside, he saw the solid earth swing up upon its edge and begin revolving slowly in a plane parallel to the side of the ship.

The thought hadn't more than time to reach his brain that this was the end, when he saw that Camilla, perfectly composed though evidently excited, was pointing at something upon the ground and calling upon him to look. It had been in order to look, he realized, that she had turned the airplane up on edge and was flying it around in a tight circle.

There were two tiny human figures down there, recognizable as men but not more particularly than that. One, moving along a path in the direction of the river, stopped to look up at the plane; the other, some distance away from him, rushed out from the cover of one clump of bushes across a clear space toward another clump fifty yards away, perhaps, though it was hard to guess from up here. Had he been hiding and made this dash for a safer place while his hunter was staring at the sky? One might have thought it was a game, only who would be playing a game like that in this sacred enclosure? There was something odd about the hider's look, as if instead of wearing a hat he had had on some sort of bright metal helmet. He seemed to be running clumsily and heavily, though Murray reflected that from this height almost any runner would look like that.

They were able to watch him for only a few seconds. Evidently this maneuver of Camilla's couldn't be protracted longer than that, for she flattened out the plane, the earth went back to its normal position; and they were flying east once more and climbing. Presently she turned in her seat, cut off the motor and shouted a question at him. He couldn't hear what she said but thought it safe to nod yes, guessing that what she meant was should they go back and take another look. Anyhow, after sweeping around in a broad circle a mile or so in diameter this is what she did.

The maneuver wasn't nearly so terrifying the second time and he began studying the ground the moment she banked her plane. This time he had lost the hider altogether. The man he had thought of as the hunter, if this was what he was, had missed his quarry completely, for he was now walking steadily along again down the path in the direction of the river, at an acute angle, that is, to the direction the runner had taken. But just in the instant before Camilla swung the ship level again, Pete caught a glimpse of a third man, or at least of a flash of confused bright colors that looked as if it might be a man in sports clothes lying on the ground. Could it be Eric? he wondered. In the costume in which he'd frightened little Ruth yesterday afternoon?

Evidently Camilla had made up her mind that there was no use going back for a third look, for after circling the field she came down to a landing, apparently satisfactory this time, taxied up to the hangar, turned a valve handle and climbed out. Murray cast off his belt and did likewise, though rather stiffly and clumsily.

She was waiting on the ground for him, of course, long before he got down, but with a tactfulness that he'd never noted before as one of her characteristics, she refrained from offering him a helping hand.

"Thank you, my dear," he said to her. "That was a great experience." It sounded queer to be talking language like that to Camilla but they were the words that came to his tongue.

She was looking up at him eagerly, but soberly too.

"I shouldn't have snapped you into that vertical bank the way I did without any warning. That must have given you quite a jolt. But things looked so queer down below there for a minute that I did it without thinking."

"You didn't recognize anybody, I suppose."

"I imagine," said Camilla, "that the man walking down the path was Mossop, or one of his boys. He usually has somebody down by the river on Sundays to see that sightseers from the field or in boats don't get into the grounds that way. The fat man who ran away I couldn't make out at all. Did you see what he had on his head? It shone like a heliograph. Did you see him the second time?"

"No. Did you?"

She nodded. "He was lying across the wall on his stomach, squirming around for a drop on the outside. I couldn't make out how he'd got up there but I suppose he'd found a ladder one of the gardeners had been using to trim the trees. It was probably no one but some curious idiot trying to get a view of the scene of the murder when he saw Mossop coming and gave him the slip. But it did look queer for a minute."

"How about the third man?" Murray asked. "Did you think you recognized him?"

Camilla's eyes widened. She hadn't seen any third man.

"Lying on the ground," Pete said. "—Or that was how he looked—not far from where the fat man started to run away, half hidden by a bush. I only caught a gleam of white and orange."

"That sweater—and those shoes?" she guessed. "Did you think it was Eric?"

He nodded.

"Bill!" she called to the mechanic who was coming toward them from the hangar. "Hang on to a wing for me, will you? I'm going to hop off again.—No, not you," she added as Murray turned back toward the plane. "Go and shed your 'chute and then drive the car home for me. We may want it for something.— There's no *danger*, Pete. Whatever the man had done, I saw him getting away. But there's no use wasting twenty minutes that might count."

Even if he could have thought of a dissuasive argument he wouldn't have been able to make it, for she was back in the cockpit now, the engine caught with a roar, and she was off.

CHAPTER IX

EXPECTING COMPANY

THANKS to the Sunday crowds that were already choking the roads, particularly the narrow cross-road from the airport to the highway, it took Prentiss Murray twenty minutes, just as Camilla had prophesied it would, to get back in her car to the Lindstrom gates, and it had seemed twice as long.

If the girl had actually seen the stout man with the shiny head wriggling across the wall and dropping down on the outside, it was hard to imagine any specific danger that could be lying in wait for her when she dismounted from her plane on the lawn before her house, though in the situation they were living in, with the shadows of their unsolved mystery lying so thick over everything, the margin from which the unforeseeable might always emerge was unusually wide.

Anyhow, it wasn't purely a doubt about Camilla's safety that worried Pete and made the traffic delays seem an insufferable affront. He had been heavily let down. The fine thrill of his flight with her had been spoiled by her going off and leaving him as a hundred and eighty pounds of excess baggage—well, she did want her car back of course; but then, she could have sent Nelson after it—when she went to confront what might be another tragedy: her brother desperately wounded, perhaps, or murdered outright.

The gates were locked, of course—they had to be on Sunday—but Murray was spared an encounter with little Ruth for it was Nelson himself who answered his ring. His manner was composed enough; evidently he had heard no terrible news within the last few minutes.

"Get in the car with me when you've locked the gate," Murray said, "and drive up to the house. Then you can take the car back."

They saw as they rounded the curve of the drive Camilla's airplane standing on the lawn. She'd landed without mishap, anyhow. A moment later he saw Camilla herself, Camilla and Eric sitting peacefully in two deck-chairs just beyond the corner of the house, enjoying cigarettes, the scattered sections of the Sunday newspaper lying about them on the grass, all as normal and contented as though no such thing as tragedy existed. Apparently Eric was in one of his agreeable moods, for the first sound Pete heard from them was Camilla's laugh.

There was nothing agreeable about his own mood

at the moment. It annoyed him that she should laugh. He didn't like the Oriental way in which she was sprawling in those damned blue trousers of hers in the deck-chair. He didn't like the way Eric was looking at her, though he had the grace to recognize that this was preposterous. A young sister like Camilla, unseen for eight years, would be a rather exciting discovery.

She gave Pete a rather intent look as he came into view, and with the purpose, he thought, of forestalling anything he might say, remarked, "Eric's rather shocked because I flew my ship in here. He says he thinks it's just as bad as keeping the pig in the parlor." She hadn't told him, then, what they had seen and thought they had seen from the air.

Perhaps it was just as well. The man lying under the bush couldn't have been Eric, anyhow, unless he'd changed his clothes again, and he wouldn't have had time for that, would he? Not before Camilla got back, certainly. He was dressed now in a well-worn blue flannel blazer with brass buttons and white flannel trousers.

Eric admitted that he had been rather shocked at finding a bit of modernity like an airplane sitting on the sacred turf. "I thought for a minute," he added, "that

I saw the old gentleman's ghost hovering over it, quivering with rage, but I suppose it was only the heated air from the engine."

Camilla looked troubled. "He did hate them," she said soberly, "—and it's so soon; only four days since . . . Pete, shall I fly it back now? You could drive the little car back to the field and bring me home."

Murray didn't respond instantly to this suggestion. Eric's joke, like all of his jokes about his grandfather, had been in offensively bad taste, he felt. Besides, he wasn't much inclined to spend another half-hour squirming through that jam of traffic in the roads. But Eric relieved him of the necessity of saying anything.

He reached out one of his fine negligent hands and patted Camilla's knee. "I didn't mean it, sister," he said. "You must learn not to take me so seriously. Now that I have become accustomed to it I rather like the idea of having the thing standing there right at the front door ready to go anywhere at a moment's notice. —Besides," he added, "I think it will amuse our guest."

"Guest?" questioned Camilla, sitting up straight.

"My friend Taylor," he explained, "who telephoned last night when I was in too bad a temper to come down and talk to him. He called again this morning and I invited him out for dinner and to spend the night."

There was a rather blank silence for a minute. Camilla must have been seeing things last night, Pete reflected, or at least misinterpreting in the light of her superheated imagination what she did see, for there was no trace of anything now but mild amusement in her brother's manner.

Evidently she thought so too, for she dropped back in her chair again and said indifferently, "Dinner? He'll have to get here pretty soon, then. What time did you ask him for?"

Her brother's manner chilled a little. "I asked him for seven," he said. "Why not?"

"Because dinner's at one," she told him. "In about half an hour. Eric, you *can't* have forgotten the one o'clock Sunday dinner!"

He laughed. "Good Lord, no! But I had forgotten it was Sunday."

"I could ask the cook and Sophy to stay in, I suppose," said Camilla doubtfully, "though they might think I was trying to start something and that now was the time to make a stand. Mrs. Smith used to get us our Sunday night suppers, you see.—But perhaps Carl would do that. I'd sort of forgotten about him."

Control of her face was not one of Camilla's conspicuous talents and at the memory of what Carl's real job in the household was she blushed brightly. Eric, fortunately, wasn't looking at her.

"Oh, don't give it a thought," he said. "Taylor won't mind. As long as there's enough food of some sort he'll be satisfied. He's used to taking pot luck."

Camilla started to say something but stopped herself with a jerk. This time Eric *was* looking at her and waited, visibly intent, for her to go on. Instead of saying what had been in her mind, however, she jumped decisively to her feet and announced that she was going in to bathe and change before dinner. Also, she would drop into the kitchen and size up the prospects for supper. At the same time Pete became aware that he was feeling rather gritty and would have followed her into the house if Eric, with an indolent wave of the hand, hadn't detained him.

"Should you feel," he asked, "that I was betraying a lack of what is called proper feeling if I brought up the question of money and asked how my grandfather disposed of his? I suppose Camilla knows all about it by now but it happens I don't."

"It hasn't occurred to me to speak to her about it," Murray told him, "and I doubt if she's even thought of it. But I've no objection to telling you what I know. His official will, so to speak, was a document he and his lawyers had been at work on for years. It never was executed because he never could be satisfied with it. His wife's death upset the whole thing of course. At that time, in order that he shouldn't by any mischance die intestate he drew up a very simple makeshift will, designating considerable sums to certain charities and dividing the rest of his property equally between you and Camilla. That will's in the vault at our office, and unless he's made a later one that I know nothing about, it will control the division of the estate."

Eric drew a long breath. "Well, that was handsome of him," he remarked.

"It utterly misrepresents his intentions," Murray told him grimly. "In his search for impossible safeguards he died without taking any. Camilla will get control of her share of it before she gets her mother's —for that's in trust till she's twenty-one."

"It's always dangerous to over-reach," Eric observed philosophically. "And, if you don't mind one question more, how much, approximately, will—Camilla's share run to?"

The form of the question might have amused Murray but it didn't. "I wouldn't try to approximate it," he snapped. "It's a lot."

"Could you be any more definite as to when the first

—instalments of the lot will begin to be available?"

"There's no manner of doubt about that," Murray assured him with a grin. "There won't be any instalments. Nothing will be disbursed from the estate except to pay allowed debts and to conserve the property until the whole thing is ready to liquidate. That won't be for at least a year."

It was by mere chance that he looked into the young man's face as he said that, but what he saw there startled him. He was reminded of the look Camilla had described last night, the features composed enough but something fixed about the eyes that suggested a sudden terror; "like an animal in a corner," she had said and it didn't now seem like an exaggeration.

Murray indicated the end of the interview by getting out of his chair and saying he must go in and wash up for dinner, but a feeling more like sympathy than anything he'd so far felt for Eric kept him from walking away until he had said, "You aren't in real straits, are you?"

"Financial?" said Eric. "Oh, no; at least I don't think so. As a matter of fact I don't know how I stand —exactly."

Well, Eric *wouldn't* know; probably never in his life had known exactly.

"Go down to the bank to-morrow and talk to Howell," Pete advised him. "He'll enlighten you. If you really need money there's no doubt, of course, that you can borrow it."

Eric nodded indifferently. He seemed to have fallen into a reverie. This mood never lifted from him all through the long Sunday dinner; if anything it deepened, though the roast beef with potatoes and thick gravy and the peach shortcake may have been partly responsible. Anyhow he was so silent and so dull that it was a relief both to Pete and to Camilla when he announced as they left the table that he was going up to his room for a nap.

Murray might have felt inclined in the same direction if Camilla, who had made a very square meal indeed, hadn't announced that she was taking him for a walk. By tacit agreement they started off across the lawn in the direction of the river. They'd had no chance to talk alone together since she'd flown away from him on the field this morning, but neither of them spoke until they were well away from the house.

Pete was in a queer mood himself; queerest, perhaps, in the fact that though he was able to observe it dispassionately from outside himself and pronounce it ridiculous, he wasn't able to lift himself out of it.

Inside himself he was tenderly warming up his grievance against Camilla for having let him down this
morning; for having left him behind as excess baggage
when an emergency, or what looked like one, presented
itself. After all, though middle-aged, he was still able-
bodied. If she had found anything ugly or dangerous
waiting for her where she landed her airplane she'd
have wanted him badly.

Without going the length of wishing she had, he did
wish intensely that she might realize she *would* have
wanted him—in a different event from the one which
seemed to justify her. Perhaps that was getting rather
fine spun. Anyhow, she might see that he was feeling
hurt about something, slip her arm through his, then
take his hand and say, "Tell me the bad news, darling,
and get it off your chest," or something like that.

She was doing nothing in the least like that. She had
on one of her new long dresses, almost down to her
ankles, and a shade hat, and she was walking decor-
ously along beside him, like a young lady at a garden
party. Perhaps it wasn't quite reasonable of him to
object to this when he'd been so superior about her
blue denim trousers this morning.

She broke the silence at last by saying, "I'll be glad
when we're through with Gordon Taylor."

"Eric can't be as much afraid of him as you thought he was last night," he observed, a little more argumentatively than he meant his voice to sound. "At all events he seemed to take him calmly enough this morning."

"He lied about him this morning," said Camilla. "—or else last night. Last night he pretended not to know who he was at first. Then he said he must be a chap he'd picked up on the train. This morning he knew all about him; said he'd want a lot to eat and wouldn't care what it was as long as it was food; said he was used to taking pot luck. And he said it as if he knew, too."

"That's what you thought of, then, and didn't say, just before you went in to dress?"

She nodded. "I hate it, Pete! Holding my breath all the time, looking around to see if any one's listening; wondering what things mean. It isn't the murders, it's Eric himself. I didn't feel that way until he came back, except when I remembered that he was coming back."

"He's in trouble of some sort," Murray agreed. "Something that he's trying to settle for himself. Either he'll succeed and the thing will clear up, or he'll have to take us in on it and we'll know what it is. The only thing for us to do just now is to stand by and see what happens."

" 'For us,' " she repeated, with a stress on the pronoun. Her eyes filled and she turned and kissed him. "You're a rock of Gibraltar, Pete," she said. "I'd fly to pieces and blow away, I think, if it weren't for you."

Her kiss had thrilled him. It had been no childish caress. But he was a little chilled by her calling him a rock of Gibraltar. "Tell me what happened after you landed your plane this morning," he said.

"I'm taking you now to show you what I found," she told him. "Why, as soon as I got out of my plane and dumped my 'chute I started running the way we're going now toward the place where you thought you'd seen Eric lying under a bush."

"I did see somebody," he maintained stiffly, "and I'm still betting it was Eric."

"Wait until you hear the rest of it," she admonished him. "I'd thought at first I'd go into the house and get Carl to come down with me, but I remembered before I'd wasted any time doing that, that one of the Mossops was patrolling the river bank and I could call him if I found anything. But I didn't find a thing. Nobody on the grass; no sign that any one had been there except some pieces of dried mud a little way from the river, as if somebody had been scraping it off his shoes. That must have been the man with the shiny head that we saw running."

They were now on the scene of their aerial observation and Murray branched off to make an independent search for some trace of the man he "thought he'd seen" lying on the ground. Damn it, he *had* seen him! He wouldn't need much to confound Camilla with but he did want something, if only a burnt match or a cigarette stub. He didn't, however, find even these, and it was from mere stubbornness that he was keeping up the search when he heard her calling him, evidently excited but with triumph rather than fear.

She had made good her guess about the pruner's ladder, it appeared. The thing was leaning against the wall at a point where an encircling mass of shrubbery hid it from any view from the lawn. It had, however, been dragged, not carried, and the scraped tracks on the grass had led her to it. They also proclaimed that no gardener had put it there. Camilla had climbed it and was sitting on top of the wall, looking a good deal less, he reflected on catching sight of her, like a guest at a garden party than she had half an hour ago. "Come up," she commanded. "There's something here for you to look at."

What she pointed out to him were some muddy marks on the coping, some thin as if they'd been left by a dirty wet rag and some scrapings on the edge that looked as if a muddy shoe had deposited them there. He didn't need to have it pointed out to him that this confirmed and explained everything she'd seen from the air.

The man with the shiny thing on his head had got into the grounds by crossing the river—there were plenty of places where it could be waded at this time of year if you didn't care how deep you went into the mud—and later, though how much later they had no way of knowing, he had been frightened off by the sight of one of the Mossops. He'd found the providential pruner's ladder left standing against the tree, had taken it to this point near the wall where the shrubbery afforded concealment, climbed to the top of the wall and dropped to the outside. He couldn't have been a very muscular or active man, Camilla guessed, or he'd have carried the ladder instead of dragging it and leaving tracks.

"That's all there is to it, Pete," she argued after they had climbed down the ladder and started strolling back toward the house together. "He was some nut who was so nosey that he simply had to get inside.

Most likely another amateur detective. Nelson says they come to the gate in swarms, with all sorts of excuses for getting in, some of them quite well-dressed nice-looking people. But this one must have been more like a common tramp or he wouldn't have gone through the river. Even when it's as low as it is now he must have got into water up to his waist and in mud to his knees. I've done it and I know. Well, and when he got across he didn't know what to do next, so he just lurked around for a while and when he saw Mossop he beat it."

"You aren't accounting for the man I saw," he pointed out, "—or for whatever it was I saw that looked like a man—that I guessed was Eric."

"It wasn't Eric," she insisted. "He was up at the house all the time."

A non-responsive answer of this kind always annoyed him, even when Camilla did it. She didn't very often.

"Your story doesn't account for what I saw," he pointed out, "whether it was Eric or not. There's nothing there now that might have been the thing I saw: something in bright colors and about as big as a man. So it must either have got up and walked away or have been picked up and carried away within the ten minutes between my seeing it from the air and your coming down there on the lawn looking for Eric. Apparently you think I was so frightened by that bit of stunt flying of yours that I began seeing things that weren't there at all."

"It wasn't a stunt," she said sulkily. "It was a vertical bank."

He waited a minute for her to deny the other part of his accusation, but she didn't add a word, so he went on, getting crosser every minute. "I don't think your story makes good sense even on the assumption that I *was* seeing things. I don't believe that any man, even an amateur detective, who wanted to get in here badly enough to come across the river would have fled for his life just because he caught sight of a Mossop. He'd have dropped behind a bush and let the Mossop go by. And then he'd have stayed here until he got what he wanted. I'd be willing to bet that he *had* got what he wanted when we saw him running, and that the man I saw lying on the ground had something to do with it."

Camilla's only contribution to the conversation when he paused was to say, "I'd like to know what made his head so shiny."

Pete glared at her. "You say," he went on, in his

most intimidating court-room manner, "that Eric was in the house all the time? How do you know he was?"

"I'll tell you about that," said Camilla politely. "When I came back to the ship from hunting for his body and was looking to see how badly I'd torn up the lawn and whether the ship was dripping oil anywhere, he came strolling out of the house. And after he'd finished bawling me out for having put it down there—but rather pleasantly, you know; as though he was half in fun—I asked him if he'd just got up, and he yawned and said hardly that yet. I asked him if he'd had his breakfast and he said, yes, Carl had brought it up to him, and it was an attention he hadn't expected. And then we went and sat down in one of the deck-chairs and he asked what kind of a fly I had had, and I told him I'd taken you. And we joked a little about my taking him up some time. And then you came around the corner of the house."

They walked on in silence after that, Murray really trying to fit things together. If Eric, dressed in his golf sweater and knickers, had been lying on the ground near the bush when Camilla's airplane made its second vertical bank, would it have been possible for him to come strolling out of the house in another suit of clothes at the time testified to by Camilla? He reached the conclusion that it was possible; just about.

He was disconcerted on looking around at the girl at his side to see that she had interpreted his silence as indicating not deep thought but bad temper. Well, he had been in a temper. So had she, for that matter. But what was that to worry about? They'd been spatting and scrapping, arguing with each other and calling each other names, for years. It was nothing but a mental substitute for a physical tussle, and they both enjoyed it. They hadn't enjoyed this, though. What was the matter with them? What had made the difference? A week ago he'd have caught her up in a hard hug, kissed her emphatically and told her that even though he might have been a hyena that didn't entitle her to be an idiot. He wanted to do that now, or something like it, but he found it impossible.

She didn't speak to him again until they'd reached the house. Then she turned to him and said, "It hasn't been a very nice walk, has it, Pete? I think I'll go in," and left him sunk.

From where they had stood on the lawn he watched her go up-stairs, to her own room no doubt, and presently, following her in, he turned into the study, selected a dull book—there were plenty of them to choose from—out of the glass-fronted bookcase, and dropped into the big leather easy chair that old Mrs. Lindstrom had had made to order from such extravagantly thorough specifications and which her husband, so far as Murray knew, had never sat in. He didn't mean to read; the book was a mere protective device against Eric's coming in and talking to him. He meant to think. But he didn't do that, either. He fell almost instantly asleep.

And then there was a hand on his shoulder and a voice, Camilla's voice, in his ear. This seemed natural enough. He'd been dreaming about her. Only what she was saying now didn't fit in with the dream.

"I hate to do it, darling, but I've got to this time. Pete, wake up!"

Yes, of course. Only there was such a long way to come up from the deeps where he'd been. Something must have happened. He struggled to get up out of the damned easy chair but he was being held down. Camilla was holding him down, it seemed.

She was sitting on the arm of the chair. "It's all right," she assured him. "There's no hurry. Nothing's going to happen for a few minutes. But Gordon Taylor's coming."

He sank back contentedly enough. The cardinal

thing about his universe was right again. Camilla was sitting on the arm of his chair. "I thought the brute wasn't coming until later," he said; "—six o'clock or so."

"It's half past six," she told him. "Ruth just came up from the gate and asked if he was to be let in and I told her yes, and sent Carl up to call Eric. But there's no hurry." She settled a little closer against him by way of showing that there was no hurry. "I was all wrong this afternoon, Pete," she went on. "I guess you had it doped out pretty near right."

"I'm always right," he said lazily. "What about?"

"About Eric under the bush. He could have got back to the house while we were talking about what we'd seen, over at the field. And he could have changed his clothes while I was beating the bushes for him. As soon as I'd figured that out I asked Sophy if she'd had a chance to do his room before lunch and she said yes, right after he went out. I asked her when that was and she said it was just after we'd driven away to the field. So you see, he and the man with the shiny head could have been talking together for nearly two hours before we saw them at all. Like Macbeth and the First Murderer, you know. Then they heard Mossop coming and Eric hid and the First Murderer ran away."

Pete was startled. "What do you mean, 'First Murderer'?"

"Oh, I don't know," she said. "Only if Eric was framing it up with somebody to protect him from Gordon Taylor that would account for his not being afraid of Mr. Taylor any more—or Emil, if that's who he is. There's the car now. Pete, do you suppose it really will be Emil—disguised, you know?"

They both stood up so that they could see better. The fact that the car was an ordinary yellow taxi served, unreasonably enough, to take off the edge of their excitement a little.

"From the luggage he's bringing you'd think he meant to stay a month," Camilla observed. Besides an enormous black suitcase there appeared to be two or three smaller bags.

Some one was coming down the stairs: Carl, it sounded like.

The place where the taxi stopped under the porte-cochère was perfectly commanded by the south window in the study, so the two spectators could watch the scene, whatever it turned out to be, as easily as if it were being played on the stage. Carl had come out and stood waiting, in his best butler's manner, to receive the guest. He had his broad back to them.

As the taxi door opened and its passenger emerged, Camilla uttered something between a gasp and a laugh of relief. "It isn't Emil," she whispered to Pete. "He certainly doesn't look like Eric."

"More like two of Eric," Pete said, also in a whisper, though the noise the taxi engine was making would have covered their ordinary voices. "Apparently he doesn't like butlers; that was a dirty look he gave Carl."

He was paying the taxi driver now while Carl lifted the luggage, piece by piece, from the cab to the veranda.

"Who does the man look like, Camilla?" Pete demanded. "Does he remind you of anybody?"

He was a fattish man with small features and a pursed-up mouth.

Camilla stared at him a moment, then turned wide-eyed to Murray. "The man at the airport this morning? The 'damned fool' that Brownie told me not to kill?"

Pete nodded. She'd confirmed his own recollection.

Something else was confirmed a moment later. The man had put his change back into his pocket. Carl was taking the last of the bags out of the car. Taylor, standing in the shade and waiting for the operation to be completed, took off his heavy Panama hat and mopped his sweaty head with his handkerchief. He was as bald as an egg.

"The heliograph!" whispered Camilla. "That's why his head was so shiny."

There couldn't be any doubt about it. Immaculate as their new house guest was in his flannels and his Panama, he was the man who'd waded the river this morning, and two hours later had climbed the wall.

CHAPTER X

MURRAY couldn't make up his mind whether he accepted Camilla's theory or not. She, in characteristic fashion, had leaped to it instantly and would not allow that there was any reasonable doubt about it. According to her, the Gordon Taylor whose telephone message last night had so terrified Eric was either Emil or some ally of his entrusted with his vengeance. The man sitting here at their dinner table in the chair Hopkins had occupied last night, the man who had spent an hour or so this morning conferring with Eric in the shrubbery, still figured in her mind as the First Murderer: that is, as some one whom Eric had summoned somehow, from somewhere, either to do away with Emil in the simple Macbeth manner or at least to help stand off his expected attack.

The hypothesis had, really, a good deal in its favor. Eric had come down and greeted his guest in a perfectly natural manner—unless you wanted to object that it was too natural—cordially, for him, but without effusion and certainly with no trace of nervousness or fear. The four of them had sat for a few minutes on the lawn in the shade of the house to enjoy the cool breeze and because there was no hurry. They hadn't talked about much but the weather, except to explain to Taylor the presence of the airplane in front of the house. It had amused him, as Eric had predicted. Then Eric had taken him in to show him his room.

Eric's choice of this room for his guest was something you could get into an argument about. There were two places where the man might have been put: a suite on the top floor opposite Eric's own, and the room on the second floor which had once been poor Lucretia's. Her things, of course, had all been cleared up and packed away. It was this room that Eric had, rather decisively, chosen.

Murray thought this showed that Eric really was afraid of him and didn't want him in a place where access to himself in his sleep would be so easy. Camilla's argument was that Eric wanted his defender in a better strategic position than the third floor, where, specifically, the veranda roof under his window and the down-spout offered a chance to leave the house informally, if necessary, during the night. Well, that was about as broad as it was long.

The man had come down to dinner looking like a

prosperous gangster at a night club. They were having a regular dinner, as it happened, for Mrs. Rosnes and Sophy, upon not being asked to stay in, had declared their entire willingness to do so and had exerted themselves to produce a real company meal. None of the family had dressed for it, of course; not even Eric. But Mr. Gordon Taylor had appeared, somewhat to their consternation, in a superbly tailored tuxedo and a diamond stud. He wasn't in the least embarrassed about so outshining them, either; he seemed, on the contrary, very well pleased with himself over having done conspicuously the right thing. There was an exciting-looking bulge under his coat which gave out a deeply muffled metallic sound on colliding with the back of his chair when he sat down to dinner, but this proved before the meal was over to be not a revolver but a flask.

He got it out hospitably when he found his hosts weren't providing anything of the sort and offered it round, beginning with Camilla. She declined, and so, a little to their surprise, did Eric. Pete, to save the man's feelings, accepted and found that it was as good whisky as its producer had boasted. Once this point of etiquette was settled, Taylor devoted himself for the rest of the meal impartially to the food, the whisky and Camilla. When he had finished the food and the whisky, he devoted himself exclusively to Camilla.

Well, there it was. Whether an enemy of Eric's or an ally he was clearly no one that Camilla's brother could ever, in the wildest cast of his folly, have made friends with. If he hadn't blackmailed his way in here for some purpose of his own then Eric had invited him only to stave off some more dangerous visitor. His fatuous belief that he was playing the gentleman in a brilliant manner and fascinating Camilla made Murray long to kick him out of the house without more ado. It gave him a very queer feeling indeed to realize that this could not be done without the gravest danger to all of them. The man probably carried his revolver where it *didn't* show in a bulge under his coat.

At the end of the meal when Carl asked Camilla where they would have their coffee she said, after a moment's hesitation, "In the study," adding explanatorily to Murray and Eric, "It's the coolest room in the house to-night." She was, Pete saw, carrying out a deliberate resolution to live the tragedy down.

But Taylor said, genially, as he followed her to the door, "That's the room where 'X' marks the spot, isn't it? Where the old gentleman got drilled, you know."

Camilla had a perfectly steady answer ready for him but she was interrupted in making it by an unexpected tantrum of Eric's. He was the last of them to enter the study, and walking around behind the easy chair where Pete had had his nap that afternoon, he stumbled over something, picked up the offending object, glared at it—it was nothing more exciting than the eighth volume of Mitford's *History of Greece* in full morocco—started, apparently, to ask who in the hell had left that lying around but broke the sentence in the middle in sheer speechless childish fury with a sweeping stare around the room.

Murray apologized coldly. "I got it out, to fall asleep over, this afternoon. Sorry I left it lying on the floor. I don't believe it's injured, though." He took it from Eric's shaking hand and restored it to its place in the bookcase.

Eric had apparently no apology to offer on his part. He always sulked a while after he'd lost his temper. So Camilla, turning quietly to Taylor, answered his question as if nothing had happened.

"Grandfather wasn't shot in this room," she explained, "but on the little staircase that goes up behind that door to his room that's right above this. That's the room where his secretary, Miss Parsons, was killed."

With a paralyzing coolness Taylor interpreted the girl's words as permission to look about a bit for himself. He opened the door to the little staircase, stepped up on the landing, looked about, came back and subjected the whole room to a good-humored inquisitive stare like that of a tourist being shown the sights of the Tower of London.

"The papers said something about a safe," he remarked. "I suppose it's in there under the stairs," and interpreting their frozen silence as consent to further prying, he pulled open the square door in the paneling that masked the safe and beamed at it in satisfaction with his own acuteness. "I noticed," he went on, "that the papers didn't say how much the guy that did this job got away with; something pretty good, wasn't it?"

He'd asked the question of Camilla but she turned helplessly to Murray and he spoke for her. "You'll have to go to the police for any information of that sort," he said.

Taylor apologized voluminously. He'd meant no offense he was sure, and they were perfectly right to keep it dark, especially if any serious loss had been involved.

There was a diversion here. Sophy appeared at the

door into the hall, looking very distracted and upset, to ask if she might speak a word to Miss Camilla. Camilla went to the door, and then perceiving that the maid's communication required more privacy than this afforded, walked away with her toward the back of the house. It was a relief to Murray to have her out of the room, if for no other reason than that her withdrawal displeased Taylor.

Presently he got going again, however, addressing himself now to Murray and paying no attention whatever to Eric, who since his first outburst of anger had sat, flushed and sulky, without speaking a word. Taylor's line now was tolerant ridicule of the police, especially detectives, and most especially self-proclaimed experts. They messed around, he said, and cackled like a lot of hens over pretended clues, most of which they'd planted themselves, but these college boy tricks never got them anywhere. Murray, having come to the easy resolution to give nothing away, not even so much as might be found in the most perfunctory phrase of agreement or consent, listened comfortably enough, relaxed in his chair, his face expressionless.

Eric, though, was evidently being goaded to the limit of endurance by his guest's talk, and finally sprang to his feet. "Taylor and I have got some business to talk about," he explained to Murray. "I think we'll say good night and go up-stairs."

"That's O. K. with me," said Taylor. "I can talk one place just as well as another."

The only sinister thing about that remark lay in the words themselves; the manner in which they were spoken was innocent enough. Yet Eric visibly flinched at them and hurried his guest out of the room. Ally or not, Eric hated him, Pete was convinced, from the bottom of his soul.

It was a relief to hear Camilla coming back. She reappeared in the doorway so promptly after the men had left the room as to suggest that she'd been lying low somewhere waiting for them to go. He held out his hand to her by way of inviting her in and indicating that the coast was clear, but she shook her head.

"It isn't nice in there," she said. "The room hasn't got over him yet. Come on outdoors. It's a good sort of night."

So he walked with her out on to the lawn and then asked her, wondering whether any new horror was impending over them, what had been the matter with Sophy.

But she could manage a laugh about Sophy. "They're having fits out there in the kitchen," she told him, "—

Sophy and Mrs. Rosnes—about Carl. They told me, with their eyes sticking right out of their heads, that he must be a burglar or something. When he cleared off the table after dinner he didn't bring all the silver out to the pantry to be washed; part of the knives and forks and spoons were missing, and a couple of drinking glasses, too, which sounded silly even to Sophy. And then, just when he ought to have been helping, he disappeared for about twenty minutes and they saw him come sneaking back from around the corner of the greenhouse.

"I didn't know exactly what it meant myself but I saw I had to take it seriously so I told them to keep it dark from Carl that they suspected anything and that when Mr. Hopkins came in the morning we'd tell him about it. I suppose they'll bolt themselves into their room and keep a light going all night in order not to be murdered. But of course I couldn't explain that he was a cop. Pete, what do you suppose he *did* want the silver for and the glasses?"

"Finger-prints, I guess," he told her. "It's a pretty good bet that Taylor's got a police record, and if he has they may give us a line on him."

He could feel her shivering as she clung to his arm, but when he made a move to lead her back into the house she balked. "I don't want to go in," she protested. "It's horrible in there. The whole place is horrible. I knew it would be like that when Eric came home but not that it would be as bad as this."

"You needn't go in," Pete told her, struck by a sudden idea. "There's no reason why you shouldn't spend the night in my flat. Williams and his wife will look after you. We'll rout out Nelson now and have him drive you in.—Why, what's the matter with that?"

For, though she'd greeted the opening of this suggestion with an ecstatic little gasp of assent, before he'd finished she'd pulled her arm out of the embrace of his and stood confronting him in a fine young rage. "Pete, you idiot!" she cried. "Did you think I'd go off alone and leave you here?"

"Did you think," he demanded in turn, "that I meant to go off with you and leave Eric to be murdered by that gunman? Oh, we don't know," he conceded in the next breath, "that that's what he's here for. Maybe you're right that he's a body-guard. But something ugly is getting ready to happen and it may happen to-night. How would I feel if it did happen while I was safely spending the night with you at my flat in town?—And how would I look?" he added unwisely.

"You're rather vain of your looks, aren't you?—your moral looks, I mean."

There was a real sting in this and he turned away from her sharply.

But the next instant she was hugging him and crying, with her face buried in his coat. "What's the *matter* with us, Pete?" she wanted to know. "We used to fight all the time without hurting each other a bit and now we can't."

"I don't know," he told her unhappily. "At least, I've got a sort of idea that I do know but I'm not equal to trying to explain it to-night."

"Well, you were right about this," she said when he'd given her a handkerchief to wipe her wet face with. "We can't run away, either of us. Only I wish we didn't have to go into the damned house. I wish we could roll up in a couple of blankets and sleep out under a tree."

"There's the west veranda," he suggested; "the hammock for you and the long chair for me. I'll go and get some blankets and we can stay there as late as you like; until sunup, unless your own bed begins to seem inviting to you before that."

She kissed him in her old manner and dispatched him for the blankets.

He went to his own room for them, remembering a traveling rug that would serve for himself and a big down comforter that would be just the thing for Camilla; also he thought he might as well change his shoes for a pair of soft slippers and his coat for a cardigan jacket.

While he was so occupied Carl knocked on his door and brought in a pitcher of ice-water on a tray. Beside the pitcher lay a note, a rather surprising note, from Hopkins, from whom they hadn't heard a word that day. "Things are coming to a head all right," the message ran. "Carl will spend the night on the third floor keeping watch on Mr. Lindstrom's room. Your job is to look after Miss Camilla. Don't start anything if you can help it, but in an emergency ring Nelson's bell. That will bring us within a minute." Carl, who had waited in silence for him to read it, now took it back and put it in his pocket, the action contrasting oddly with the perfect butlerian manner in which he said, "Thank you, sir. Good night, sir."

Apparently Hopkins agreed with Camilla. The implications in the message were formidable enough but Pete's own orders warmed his heart. He'd look after Camilla, all right.

It surprised him to hear her moving about in her

room and he went to the connecting door and tapped on it softly. She came and opened it wide enough to talk through. "Changing your mind?" he asked.

"No, my clothes," she said. "I got an idea. Wait for me a minute and I'll go down with you."

It was hardly longer than that before she came into his room in those blue denim trousers of hers and a white sweater. She took half his load of blankets and they stole down together to the veranda.

It was easy to guess what her idea was: another flight in the airplane as soon as it got light enough to take off. Evidently, though, she was saving it up as a surprise for him for she didn't mention it. She went straight to her hammock and asked him to cover her up. "Eric and the First Murderer seem to have gone. to bed," she said, "so we'd better get what sleep we can while the sleeping's good."

She wasn't, though, quite done with him yet for she murmured when he bent over her to kiss her good night, "It would be awfully nice and exciting if you'd try to explain what it is that's the matter with us that makes us so we can't fight any more—but of course you won't until you get good and ready."

He sat there on the edge of the hammock where she lay, staring blankly down into the face he had just kissed. Her eyes held him somehow and he felt himself suddenly breathless.

"Oh, Pete, don't look so *terrified*," she said. "Good night, darling."

A chair, no matter how comfortable, is a dreadful thing to get to sleep in, unless you are trying to keep awake, and Prentiss Murray, between the possibilities for reflection latent in that last remark of Camilla's and the vague expectation that some time before morning the deep night silence was going to be torn by a shot or a scream, looked forward to nothing better than sitting broad awake until dawn, at least.

It was pleasant, though, and rather relaxing to watch Camilla. There was a good moon well up over the house and the gentle diffusion of its light enabled him to see her quite well. No kitten could have gone to sleep more promptly and confidently than she did: a stretch, a yawn, a protesting little wriggle until she could find the position that suited her, and she was off as if there weren't a care or a danger in the world. Apparently there wasn't, for her, so long as she had him close beside her like this on guard. He felt pleasantly guilty about this reflection for a few minutes—a very few—and then he betrayed her trust by falling fast asleep himself.

The next thing he knew it was broad daylight, though still very early since the sun was just beginning to gild the grass. That robin, or some similar bird—he couldn't see it; only hear it—must have been what had waked him up. Otherwise everything was quiet. Camilla, still sound asleep, lay there in the hammock, only not just as he had left her. Evidently she'd got too warm during the night for she'd not only thrown off her comforter, she'd stripped off her white sweater and all she had on beneath it was a little pink silk undershirt.

The sight of her simply entranced Pete and he was gazing half hypnotized when she suddenly opened her eyes and looked at him with a lazy little good-morning smile. Idiotically his eyes filled with tears so that he had to turn away and blink. He didn't know whether she had noticed this or not. She sat up unconcernedly, stretched her arms high above her head, yawned, and finally remarked, "Well, it's morning, and I don't believe anything's happened. Listen, Pete! Can't you hear the First Murderer snoring up there in his room?"

Pete listened and thought he could, for a fact. He wished the devil Camilla would put on her sweater. She was lovely like this but it simply wasn't decent.

She patted the hammock and said, "Come over here where we can talk."

"Don't you think . . ." he began.

But she caught on before he had got any further than that, which was lucky, since he'd felt utterly incapable of saying it. She flushed, looked for a minute as if she might throw something at him, and then meekly pulled the garment on over her head. Whereupon he came and sat down where she had patted the hammock.

But their greeting was spoiled, somehow. "There we are again, Pete," she remarked. "Something's got to be done about this. If you didn't like the way I looked why didn't you say, 'Damn it, Camilla, you can't go around naked! Put on that sweater!'?"

He recognized his idiom all right and grinned over it but he had to admit that he couldn't seem to talk that way to her any more.

"Well," she proceeded, "come along with your explanation. You said you had one last night. This is serious, Pete. Let's have your idea of what's the matter with us."

He began cautiously. "You're getting older; growing up. Really, I guess that about covers the ground."

"Marvelous, Holmes!" she put in, and derailed him entirely. "You mean it's all my fault, then," she went on. "You must mean that, because *you* aren't growing up. You haven't changed a hair since I can remember. Pete, how much longer are you going to be my guardian?"

"I'm not your guardian!" he snapped, since the question had irritated him. "I'm the guardian of your property until you're twenty-one. But you aren't a minor. Anyhow, you're of age in Illinois."

She seemed astonished at this information. "I can do anything I like?—Oh, you know what I mean." She must have perceived that he meant to tell her nobody could do whatever they liked. "Get married, for instance, without your consent?"

"Get *married!*" he echoed. Then he pulled himself together. "Yes, of course."

She seemed skeptical about this. "You could reduce my allowance, though, couldn't you? Cut me off with a shilling, or something like that?"

"No," he said, "I couldn't even do that. I'm obliged to pay you a reasonable allowance; whether I liked the man you married or not wouldn't make a particle of difference." Then, though he knew all the time he was being a fool, he asked, "Camilla, *is* there anybody?" He was thinking again about that pilot over at the field.

[244]

"Sure there is," she said. "But you don't have to worry. I proposed to him night before last and he turned me down flat."

There was a bewildered minute before he could remember when night before last was and see what she meant. Then he glared at her. "I thought we were talking seriously," he said.

"We are," she told him steadily. "A lot more seriously than you'll admit. Let's quit stalling, Pete. I've meant to marry you ever since I was eleven years old. That was just luck, because of course I didn't know anything much, then. Not enough to go on. But I know enough now. I'm in love with you, all right. You're in love with me, too, aren't you? Isn't that what's the matter with us?"

There was a petrified silence which seemed to last for hours. Then he admitted miserably, "Yes, it is."

"Well, then," she asked, still holding herself pretty steady, "what's the matter with that?"

"It's outrageous, that's what's the matter with it," he burst out. "I'm more than twice as old as you. You ought to marry somebody young; not an elderly 1915 model half worn out . . ."

"Shut up!" she cut in fiercely. "Pete, I'm not a blue-eyed baby. I've been kissed and pawed by enough wet smacks to know what I don't like. And I know what I do like, too. I'm in love with you, and I know what it's all about."

He was feeling a little as he'd felt the first time she'd taken him into that vertical bank in her airplane; only this was worse. His whole spiritual cosmos was turned up on edge and spinning around. Phrases were going through his head about his position of trust, and taking advantage of her youth, but they all seemed too imbecile to say. He didn't say anything. He just sat there looking at her.

He still couldn't say anything, even when he could see that her strong self-control was beginning to give way and that a panic was gripping her. With a sudden new dignity that terrified him she got up from the hammock.

"I guess I've had about all I can stand of this, Pete," she said; "for one morning, anyhow. I'm going out to fly the little ship around for a while. Will you come and wind up the self-starter for me? I'm going in the house for a minute to get my 'chute."

He spent his two or three minutes of grace beside the airplane in a desperate effort to force his mind to start functioning again as a mind and not as a humming top, but he could make no headway with it. All he could think of to say when she came out of the house in her clumsy harness was, "Take me with you, Camilla."

She shook her head. "No 'chute," she explained. "We'll get you one to-day if you like and keep it here to have it handy."

There was nothing for him to do after that but grind the crank she'd pointed out to him and stand clear of the propeller and then wait for a wretched quarter of an hour, unable to speak above the roar of her infernal engine, while it was warming up. At last she nodded, gave him a smile of sorts and a wave of the hand, released her brakes and let her airplane roll forward over the lawn. A minute more and she had cleared the trees.

He became conscious of the want of a bath, a shave and fresh clothes; perhaps they would help pull him together. He'd got to get himself together somehow before Camilla came back to breakfast. He wasted as much time as he could over the processes of his toilet, and apparently this treatment was efficacious since before he was half through shaving he found himself composing the speech he was going to make Camilla the next time they had a chance to talk together.

He must make his position clear to her. The foundation of it, the bedrock upon which the foundation rested, was the fiduciary nature of a lawyer's profession. Even his ordinary clients' affairs were a sacred trust to be dealt with always to the client's interest and never to his own. When his client was also his ward, the obligations of the trust become even more sacred. Primarily, of course, his guardianship was concerned over her property. Yet it was his moral obligation to treat her affection for him and her confidence in him as a trust equally sacred, as something it was unthinkable that he should appropriate to his selfish advantage. She was extremely young, she was, comparatively at least, inexperienced. He couldn't possibly marry her without looking like a crook.

Quite a satisfactory burst of silent eloquence, this was, until the face he saw in the shaving mirror reminded him of something Camilla had said during their quarrel of last evening: "You're vain of your looks, aren't you?—your moral looks, I mean." The recollection shattered his whole argument like a charge of dynamite.

The business of the day was at last beginning. People were stirring in the house. It was beginning over at the airport, too. Student pilots in their planes were droning over the house. Every time he heard one of them he went to the window and looked out in the hope that it might be Camilla coming down to a landing on the lawn. He wished she would come back. If her state of mind was anything like his she shouldn't be trying to fly; in her mood of reckless preoccupation anything might happen to her.

When he had worked himself into a state of acute terror about her by dwelling on thoughts like this, he went down to the study and telephoned the airport. It wasn't a sensible thing to do but it was something.

Surprisingly they were able to give him some information about her. She'd come in only about ten minutes ago to fill up with gas and had only just taken off. Well, this meant, anyhow, that she wasn't so lost to common prudence as to try to fly with an empty tank.

More comfort was waiting for him when he left the study: the sight of Taylor's luggage piled neatly just inside the front door. The man really was going away this morning. Thank the Lord for that, anyhow! Had he brought down that mountain of stuff just for an overnight stay, or had he counted on a longer visit and had Eric, somehow, found the means of getting rid of him?

Sophy, looking rather puffy about the eyes and very scared and solemn, came out to tell him that breakfast was ready, and he decided not to wait for Camilla's return. Anyhow, he'd rather be fortified by a cup of coffee or two before he had to confront her again.

Taylor, already at the breakfast table, very pink and plump, and heavily perfumed, was a phenomenon he hadn't reckoned upon, however, and he had to suppress an impulse to bolt at sight of him. Where the devil was Eric? Why couldn't he have come down to speed the parting of this abominable guest of his? Taylor had improved overnight, though, in one respect: he wasn't talkative. He seemed, indeed, rather deeply preoccupied, and Murray was permitted to sip his coffee and crunch his toast in comparative silence. It did get mentioned that this was another fine day and that Taylor was sorry to leave but expected to come back for another visit soon.

When Carl came in with Murray's eggs he had also a message for Taylor, that Nelson would be at the door for him in about ten minutes. Apparently their guest was going away in state in the limousine.

"Where's Mr. Lindstrom?" Murray asked Carl. "Isn't he coming down?"

Taylor betrayed no interest in this question, nor in Carl's answer to it.

"No, sir," the perfect butler said. "I'm to take his breakfast up to him—a little later."

No sign yet of Camilla. Well, that was all to the good. Murray hoped now that she wouldn't turn up until this fellow was clear of the place.

Nelson came with the car before they'd finished breakfast, and as they walked out into the hall together, Taylor whirled upon Murray and upon Carl, who'd followed them, to ask with a sudden cold gleam of excitement in his fat face, "What in hell's been done with my bags?"

"They're already in the limousine, sir," Carl told him suavely. "They're quite safe."

But Taylor, catching up his Panama off the hall table, strode out to see for himself. And it amused Murray, who followed, to observe that he looked them all over carefully and suspiciously before he was satisfied that none of his belongings had been tampered with. What the devil was one supposed to do in a case like this? Murray wondered. Shake hands with the crook?

Oddly enough, Nelson saved him from having to decide this question of etiquette. "Will you ride down as far as the gate with us, sir?" he asked Murray. "There's a party there who says he wishes to speak to you."

This seemed rather queer but he decided not to question it. So he followed Taylor into the car and sat down beside him.

They'd rolled perhaps half-way to the gate when the abruptly truncated roar of an airplane engine made Murray stick his head out of the open window of the car and look up. Thank the Lord Camilla had timed it exactly right! Her little green airplane swooped down over the tops of the trees, took ground and rolled up the lawn to a stop right in front of the house. Taylor going; Camilla safely back: things were straightening out again.

The car had reached the gate. Neither Mrs. Nelson nor little Ruth had been on the job, apparently, to open it for them for Nelson was getting down from the wheel to do it for himself. Queer he hadn't waited a minute and sounded his horn. The door on Murray's side of the car was pulled open and Walsh, the motor-cop, was standing there. Was it Hopkins who had sent for Murray?

But Walsh wasn't looking at him. He had a heavy automatic in his hand and he was pointing it straight at the fat belly of the man who sat beside him. "Put up your hands, Taylor," he said, "and come out!"

Whatever else for a split fragment of a second Taylor might have thought of doing with either of his hands, he decided almost as quickly that it was no use trying. He held them up as Walsh had commanded, and lumbered out of the car.

Another policeman—there were a lot of them about; half a dozen sprang up, apparently from nowhere but probably from the cover of Nelson's cottage—another policeman came up behind Taylor and began searching him, patting his sides and hips expertly while Walsh kept him covered with his gun. There was no expression whatever in the plump face. He said in an even voice, "There's nothing on me; not even a flask. I left mine with Lindstrom; thought he wanted it more than I did."

Apparently he spoke the truth. They found no weapon on him, nor anything else they wanted, and Walsh nodded to him that he might put his hands down. He continued, however, to keep him covered with the gun, and ordered him, when he would have moved off a little, to stay where he was. Evidently Taylor wanted to see what they were doing with his bags. Nelson had taken them all out of the car and disposed them, under Hopkins' instruction, along the grass as if for a customs examination.

Murray now got out of the car. Hopkins nodded to him, but with the air, Murray thought, of one who didn't want to answer any questions.

"Keys!" he said to Walsh, before even trying to see whether the bags were locked.

Taylor produced a little leather book of them and gave them up without visible reluctance, though he said, in his level expressionless voice, "I'd hate to be in your shoes if you're trying to pull this without a warrant."

"What's that you said about shoes?" was all the answer the Chief made, but curiously enough it silenced Taylor. Indeed, it did more than that: it took the color out of the pink cheeks and caused his eyes suddenly to look sick.

It was the big black suitcase that Hopkins seemed most interested in. His hands were trembling a little as he sought and found the right key and then tugged at the leather straps. Murray watched, fascinated, when he threw back the lid, and then stared incredulously from the contents of the bag to the face of the man above it. The bag simply was full of shoes—a dozen pairs at least. Apparently it contained nothing else. And Hopkins' face, gazing at those shoes, was radiant with triumph.

He picked up one of them, scrutinized the label inside, and held it up for Murray to see. "French shoes," he said. "Eric Lindstrom's." He ran his hand into it as if exploring for something and took it out, unsatisfied. It was a left shoe and he picked out a right one, ran his hand in, and instantly withdrew it with a nod.

Taylor couldn't see what he was doing, of course, but he'd heard what Hopkins said. "What if they are his shoes?" he asked truculently. "He gave them to me. Let's see your warrant, if you've got one. If I'm wanted, what am I wanted for?"

Hopkins answered without straightening up or even looking at him. "You're wanted," he said, "for complicity in the murder of Eric Lindstrom!"

Chapter XI

BACK TO EARTH

"For complicity in the murder of Eric Lindstrom!"

These were common words, grammatically strung together, but to Murray they simply refused to make sense. Some automatic tract in his mind was chewing them over dully. Murder of Eric Lindstrom. Carl's watch, then, had been unavailing. Taylor had got around him somehow.—Yet this wasn't what Hopkins had said. Why had he talked about complicity? What accomplices could the man have had? Who had been the actual murderer?

These thoughts were nothing more than the involuntary reflexes of a lawyer's mind. Except for these twitchings it was paralyzed by an unexplained terror, a nightmarish, panic sort of thing that was urging him to turn and run, wildly, desperately, toward the house; toward Camilla. To steady himself against this impulse he forced himself to watch what was happening under his eyes. The shoes weren't all that Hopkins wanted. The search was going on methodically through the rest of Taylor's baggage.

[256]

Taylor couldn't see what they were doing. The automobile was in the way and they wouldn't let him move. His face was no longer a face but a mask in papier-mâché; as expressionless as that and about that color.

Hopkins had found a small toilet case that had a false bottom to it. Razors, brushes and bottles were being dumped out on the grass so that this false bottom could be lifted.

"Here we are!" Hopkins said. From one of his pockets he took a little memorandum book bound in dark-red polished leather; with his other hand he lifted out of the toilet case three packages of yellow-backed bills; the old-fashioned large-size bills. He summoned Murray with a nod to take them from him.

"This is what I wanted you down here for," he explained. "My guess is that you'll find twenty-four thousand nine hundred dollars in these bundles, but don't try to count them now. Just check the numbers of two or three of them with the numbers in the book and make a note of them so that you can swear to them." He turned back to continue his search but it was apparent now that he had found everything he wanted.

"Quite a smart little college boy detective, aren't

you!" said Taylor. His face hadn't come to life at all but his voice had a curious corrosive quality, a distillate of boiling rage. "Sherlock Holmes and all that! Working it all out by algebra! Why, you God damned copper, you never found a thing in your life that you weren't tipped off to."

"Have it your own way," Hopkins told him good-naturedly, "but I wouldn't talk too much if I were you. Anything you say may be used against you, you know—though I don't believe we need a thing that you can tell us."

Murray had done all Hopkins wanted him to about the bills: he had found three of them whose serial numbers corresponded with three numbers in Oscar Lindstrom's memorandum book and made a notation to that effect in his own. This done, he handed the three packages to Hopkins who put them back in their hiding-place, gathered up and returned the stuff he had emptied out on the grass, locked the bag and turned to the prisoner.

"Put handcuffs on him and take him to the station. Hanson, you go with him; I shall want Walsh here. Miss Lindstrom won't mind, will she," he asked Murray, "if we use her car for a patrol-wagon?"

"No," said Murray, "I'm sure she won't."

One of the policemen, with Taylor handcuffed to his wrist, clambered somewhat sheepishly into the big Rolls-Royce and another of them started to open the gate. "That disposes of the preliminaries, I guess," said the Chief. "Now we're ready for Emil."

The Chief's voice hadn't risen but it had a knife-like quality that stabbed its way into Murray's consciousness. Emil! What did he mean? Suddenly Murray thought he knew what he meant and the sweat felt cold on his forehead.

Hopkins had finished his instructions to two of the policemen, who now set out briskly through the shrubbery in the direction of the house. He looked at his watch and turned to Murray with a question. "Camilla's out flying this morning, isn't she?"

"She was," said Murray, out of a dry throat, "but she's come in. She landed in front of the house just as we drove away from it."

You could see Hopkins didn't like this, although he said, "It'll be all right, anyway. But *you* come up to the house with us and make it your first job to find her. Take her out of the way and keep her out of the way until it's all over."

The words were almost obliterated by the sudden roar of an airplane engine and yet there was no airplane in the sky. "Turn that car around," Hopkins shouted to Nelson, "and drive up to the house! Damn it, man, never mind the grass!" He pulled open the door as the car started moving. "Climb in," he ordered. They obeyed and the car went racing up the drive.

The airplane was gone, of course. The roar they had heard had been Camilla taking off; it couldn't have been anything else. But this didn't necessarily mean anything. She might be practising landings again; she had a sort of passion for it. Or she might, seeing the house deserted, have decided to fly around for another half-hour. There was no use getting into a panic just because . . .

The car stopped with a jerk under the porte-cochère and all of them, except Hanson and his prisoner, tumbled out and rushed into the house. It was deserted, all right. There was no sign of anybody downstairs, at least, and when they stopped to listen there wasn't a sound.

Yes, there was. Up-stairs somewhere a woman was sobbing hysterically. They rushed in a clump all the way to the third floor where the noise was coming from.

Most of the sounds were being emitted by Sophy, who'd flung herself down on an old box couch which stood in the corridor and was having a well-developed fit of hysterics. Nelson's wife, the laundress, with a masterly instinct for doing the wrong thing, was petting and crying over her by turns, and paying no attention whatever to Carl who was sitting on the floor in a pool of blood, leaning for support against the side of the narrow staircase that ran up to the cupola, white-faced and, with what little strength he had left, gripping his leg just above the knee where the blood was spurting feebly from a bullet wound.

"Walsh," said Hopkins, "get a bath-towel and put a tourniquet on that leg! Nelson, make that woman stop her noise; throw water over her; drown her, if necessary."

Walsh carried out his instructions without the loss of a second, tying the bath-towel around Carl's thigh and twisting it tight with the barrel of his revolver, which was the first thing that came handy. Nelson, while this was going on, emerged reluctantly from the bathroom with a glass of water in his hand, but didn't have to throw it over anybody, for Sophy's sobs were miraculously stilled by the sight of it.

"Where's your man?" Hopkins asked Carl. "He got away from you, didn't he?"

"He got me," Carl answered drowsily. "I came up

with his breakfast and found the room empty; came out and saw him coming down from the cupola: you can see the gate from there. I'd have got him all right, but the woman screamed and warned him. He drilled me and the woman got in my way so I couldn't . . ." His voice trailed off into nothing at that point and he fainted.

They carried him into Eric's room, laid him on the bed, covered him up and got a little of the whisky from Taylor's flask, which they found on the night stand, between his lips. "He'll be all right, now the bleeding's stopped," Hopkins decided, and turned back to question the two women.

"Where did Lindstrom go?" he asked.

Sophy was speechless, merely showing signs of beginning her hysterics again. Mrs. Nelson, on the other hand, had plenty to say but she had to begin at the beginning. She seemed to feel, too, that Carl's narrative did them less than justice.

"We'd been down-stairs getting the sheets off the beds," she said, "and Sophy had just that minute been telling me how Carl was a burglar and how he'd carried off the silver from dinner last night and how Miss Camilla had told her they'd report it to you this morning. And then we came up here to get Mr. Eric's wash and we saw Carl come running out of Mr. Eric's room there with his hand on a gun that was sticking part-way out of his pocket. And there was Mr. Eric coming down from the cupola looking wild-like and not seeing Carl at all.

"Sophy yelled, 'Look out! You'll be killed!' and Carl yelled, 'Put up your hands! You're under arrest!' though what right a crook like him would have to arrest anybody I couldn't see. And then Carl fired his revolver—at least we thought it was Carl at the time—and we were trying to get out of the way when Mr. Eric gave us a push and ran down-stairs."

"You didn't follow to see where he went?"

"Me?" Mrs. Nelson seemed outraged at the idea. "Between Carl yelling and waving his gun and Sophy screaming and carrying on, I was that weak I couldn't have followed anybody."

Then came the question Pete had been holding his breath for. "When did this happen? Before you heard Miss Camilla's airplane take off from the lawn, or after?"

Mrs. Nelson couldn't say. She thought she'd noticed the noise of an airplane about that time but whether before or after she hadn't the least idea. Sophy being appealed to merely shook her head and moaned.

They were losing precious minutes and they hadn't learned a thing except how the catastrophe had happened. Hopkins allowed himself one gesture of empty-handed despair and then turned to Walsh. "I'll leave the house to you," he began. "Make sure he isn't hidden . . ." He broke off as the sound of footsteps plodding wearily and uncertainly up the stairs came to their ears.

Murray was nearest the stair head and he saw her first. "It's little Ruth," he announced. "If she's seen anything she'll be able to tell us what it is." She had seen something if the look in her face was anything to go by.

As she came up level with them both her parents started toward her, her father silently, her mother with sympathetic outcries, but Hopkins peremptorily waved them back. "Leave her to me," he said. Apparently the child was glad to see him there and glad to be left to him, for her face came to life a little and she walked over to him and took hold of his hand.

"Did you see the airplane go away just now?" he asked.

She nodded.

"Who went away in it? Any one besides Miss Camilla?"

She nodded again without speaking.

"Who was it?" he asked. "Did you think it was Mr. Eric Lindstrom?"

Something, possibly the rather peculiar way in which this question was phrased, unlocked her powers of speech. "I'll tell you," she said. "I'd been down at the river and I was coming across the lawn and I saw father drive the big car away, and it was too far for me to get to the gate so I waited. And then the airplane came over the trees and stopped in front of the house; Miss Camilla's airplane with her in it.

"She was sitting kind of humped down in her seat, and I wondered why she didn't get out. And I thought maybe if she was going up again she'd give me a ride— because she said she would some time. And I was coming up to ask her when I saw—when I saw . . .

"Well, he looked like Mr. Eric but his face was kind of horrible and he had a pistol in his hand as if he was going to shoot somebody. I was right near the steps then, nearer to him than the airplane was. I was going to scream but he looked at me and I couldn't. Camilla started to get out of the airplane but he pointed the pistol at her and she stopped, and he ran to where the airplane was, pointing the pistol at her all the time. But he called her 'Camilla, dearest' and said they were

[265]

going on some kind of voyage together and she'd better hurry because she hadn't any time to spare. He was talking the way he does, as if he was going to laugh. But he didn't laugh.

"The engine started making such a noise then that I couldn't hear anything more he said, but he climbed into the seat behind her and he kept the pistol pointed at her and shouted at her as if he was telling her to hurry. She didn't look round at him and after a while the airplane started rolling across the grass and flew away. And I felt kind of sick, so I stayed where I was, by the corner of the steps, till I saw you come in, and then I felt better."

To Murray the climax of horror in the child's recital had been the words "Camilla, dearest" that she'd quoted and the familiar manner of mockery which she'd indicated. Together they disposed of a faint doubt he'd been trying to cling to concerning the identity of this murderous Emil with the man he and Camilla had welcomed as her brother two days ago. This identity, which his mind must still reject as incredible, turned the thing into an absolute nightmare. There was no use trying to cope with it by thought or action; the best thing you could do, perhaps, was to beat yourself on the head in the hope of waking yourself up.

Hopkins didn't take it like that, though. He said to Murray, "I wish you'd go in and have another look at Carl; give him a little more whisky if you think he needs it. I'm going down-stairs to telephone. You'll find me in the study." He went, taking Walsh and Nelson with him, and the two women and the child followed him.

Murray found Carl conscious, though still half collapsed and in want of a little more whisky. Fortified by this he asked about his assailant: whether he'd got away.

"He forced Camilla at the point of a gun to fly him away in her airplane," Murray said, and Carl seemed rather pleased with the idea. Having lost your man it must, of course, be gratifying to have him reveal such resources as this instead of submitting tamely to capture at some one else's hands.

"She wants to look out where she lands him," Carl said faintly, after taking thought. "He'll try to get her to let him out in some empty field where there's nobody around. If she does that he'll kill her sure. But if she comes down with him in some regular landing field or any place where there are people around, she'll be all right. She wants to remember that."

It seemed to be Carl's idea that any good friend

of Camilla's ought to warn her at once not to overlook this important detail, and having got it off his mind he let his eyes drop shut and fell peacefully asleep.

His idea drove Murray nearly mad. It was true, of course it was true, Eric—Emil would kill Camilla as ruthlessly as any of his earlier victims to improve his own chance of escape. If he could persuade or intimidate her into making a landing in some lonely place where their descent was not observed he'd shoot her, and then perhaps set fire to the airplane. The one gleam of comfort Murray could find lay in the fact that the fugitive, coming out of the house with his revolver in his hand and compelling her under the threat of it to fly away with him, had warned her himself. If he'd pocketed his weapon and merely made a brotherly appeal to her for help she'd have gone into his trap blindly. She knew her danger now, at least.

But would the knowledge do her any good with that pistol pointed at her head from the rear cockpit? Had she any choice but to obey his orders?

His own flight yesterday enabled him to reconstruct the situation very exactly; Eric in the seat where he had sat, with Camilla's small helmeted head only far enough away to be out of reach. It wouldn't be so easy to give orders from there, though; one could give them, all right, but they wouldn't be heard.

And then suddenly, with the blinding effect of a revelation, it broke over him that the threat of that pointed pistol was a perfectly empty threat the moment the airplane got off the ground, and for as long as it stayed in the air. Of course! In that ship, at least, you couldn't kill your pilot without instantly committing suicide, unless you had a parachute. The fugitive had no parachute. Little Ruth's narrative made that clear, at all events.

Camilla might not think of that, though. It had taken him all this time to think of it. If only she could be signaled to somehow; from the ground or from another plane! Would it be possible to find her— to send a squadron of planes aloft to scour the skies for her? He got up and went down-stairs looking for Hopkins.

For some reason or other they'd brought Taylor in. He was still handcuffed to the policeman's wrist, the two of them, looking about equally disgusted, sitting side by side on a bench in the hall, and the bags were again piled neatly just inside the door as they'd been before breakfast. The study door was shut and Hanson answered Murray's inquiring look by saying that the Chief was still telephoning in there. He'd sent the chauffeur down to his own cottage to telephone for a surgeon and an ambulance for Carl, so that he might have the uninterrupted use of this instrument. Murray found a faint gleam of hopeful reassurance in the fact that the Chief had something to telephone about.

After a moment's hesitation he went into the study and closed the door behind him. He wanted to ask Hopkins whether anything could be done about organizing a search.

The Chief was listening to a report of some sort. Without speaking he nodded Murray to a chair and went on saying, "Yes," occasionally and making pencil marks on a piece of paper.

For the moment there seemed to be nothing for Pete to do but sit down and hold himself still, which in his state of desperate impatience for action wasn't easy to do. Everything he saw irritated him: the Chief's pencil marks; the fact that five of the eight big volumes of Mitford's *Greece* in full morocco had unaccountably been taken from the bookcase and were neatly piled on the desk. What the devil could any one want of five volumes of that work at once?

"Well, that covers it, I guess," said Hopkins into the phone. "I'll stay here until I get news from somewhere." He hung up and turned to Murray. "We've notified every airport within a radius of a hundred miles to try to find Camilla's ship, explaining who her passenger is and how she came to take off with him. They'll watch from the ground, of course, and they'll have planes warmed up to take off and follow her as soon as she's seen. Whoever gets on her track will stay with her and land as nearly as possible when and where she does. There are thirty-five of those airports in the area and one of them ought to pick her up." Evidently the Chief hadn't needed to be told Carl's idea.

"She'll be out of that area by now, won't she?" Murray asked gloomily.

"She hasn't got a fast ship," Hopkins answered. "It has a cruising speed of seventy-five or eighty miles an hour. And it's just,"—he pulled out his watch and looked at it—"twenty-three minutes since she took off."

"You're mad!" said Murray. "It seems hours!"

"Twenty-three minutes," reiterated the Chief. "I happened to be putting my watch back in my pocket when we heard the roar of the engine down there by the gate." He thought of something and turned to the telephone to call up the police station. "Has that ambulance started?" he asked. "Well, then, send a

stenographer along with it. I may want him.—
Ordinarily," he explained to Murray as he hung up,
"Taylor isn't the sort of man who'd talk. But he
thinks he's been double-crossed, and that on top of his
original grievance—I don't know what it was but it
must have been serious—is almost more than he can
bear."

"I thought you already knew everything he could
tell you."

Hopkins held his head. "My God, man, did you
fall for that, too? I never had a case," he went on,
"where a good whole-hearted confession would
come in handier. I've got three hard facts, but
the area of pure surmise is so big that I hate to think
about it."

The telephone rang and Hopkins snatched it up, said
who he was and listened. Murray saw his eyes widen
and his breath come in in a great deep draught. Murray held his breath, too.

"All right," Hopkins said. "You're ready for anything over there, are you? Every second will count,
you know." Apparently they—whoever and wherever
they might be—were ready for anything. Hopkins
gave a nod of satisfaction and slammed the telephone
down on the hook. Then, without pausing for a word

of explanation to Murray, he darted from the study, through the hall, and out on to the lawn.

"Start the motor in that side-car!" he was shouting to Walsh when Pete overtook him.

Then he turned to Pete. "It's Camilla! She's here! Right over her own airport; about seven thousand feet up, they say. And simply stunting hell out of her ship: doing every crazy thing it will do and some that it won't. Look, Murray! Look! Is that the ship? Can you tell?"

It was hardly more than a gleaming scrap of tinfoil in the sky. How could any one recognize it? Yet Murray felt he did. He couldn't see that it was moving at all for a minute, and then he saw that it was falling in a lazy-looking spin. His heart was in his throat before it leveled off and started climbing again. It was looping a loop now—starting one, anyhow—but right at the top it rolled over. It spiraled down and rolled over again. Which way *was* it right side up?

It kept getting nearer all the time, losing altitude with every maneuver. A terror gripped Murray. Was some horrible sort of struggle going on up there for control of the ship? Had the murderer discovered that Camilla was bringing him back to the men who were waiting to seize him and was he, in his rage, willing to risk his own death if it might involve hers?

Suddenly the struggle, if that was what it had been, was over. The plane, which had been to the west of them, above the airport, now came swooping down across the river and above the lawn as if, Murray thought, she meant to land there. Only she was coming too fast to land and too high.

"She wouldn't land down wind," Walsh shouted above the roar of her engine. He added his own contribution to the noise by opening the throttle to his motorcycle. "She's zooming the lawn for a look." He was in the saddle as the plane went by not ten feet above the level of the lawn.

Pete saw her helmeted head turn toward them and her hand flash some sort of signal. The huddled figure in the rear cockpit wasn't pointing a revolver at her now, Pete thought.

Hopkins got into the side-car as if he had understood Camilla's signal. She'd cleared the trees down by the gate, but while she was still in sight, made a vertical bank in a half-circle and turned back. The roar of her engine ceased and she was rolling up the lawn. The side-car leaped forward, overtook her, ran alongside and stopped as she did.

Pete didn't know how he got there; he must have put on a pretty good hundred-yard dash for he was only a second or two behind the motorcycle. Camilla was sitting very still in her front cockpit. She pushed up her goggles and Pete saw her turn some sort of handle that was beside her, but she didn't look around.

"Are you all right?" he heard Hopkins ask. "Did he do anything to you?"

"Not a thing," she answered him. "Be careful when you take him out, though. He's got a gun back there, if he isn't too sick to shoot it."

An exclamation from Walsh made Pete look around at the man he still thought of as Eric. His face was ghastly enough, livid and staring, the mouth open rigidly with the jaw a little to one side, but the attitude of his body was more horrible still in its stiff contortion of terror. His hands were down between his thighs as if he were clutching something.

"Put those hands up!" ordered Hopkins curtly.

But the man didn't stir nor speak.

"He seems to be fastened down somehow," Walsh observed. He'd climbed up on the wing and was looking down into the cockpit.

"Undo his safety belt," said Camilla. Still she hadn't looked around, but as she spoke she cast off her own, turned a switch that silenced the coughing engine, climbed out and busied herself getting rid of her parachute. "Don't you know how to unfasten his belt?" she asked the policeman.

"He hasn't got any belt on," Walsh answered. "He's hanging on by his hands and it seems like he can't let go: like those steel workers that get the grips and you have to pull them loose sometimes with a derrick. His hands are full of blood, too."

Pete, standing close beside Camilla, felt her lean rather heavily against him and he put his arm around her. "Faint?" he asked. "Shall I take you out of this?"

She shook her head and said she was all right.

It turned Murray rather sick to see the way Walsh had to put his back into it in order to break that convulsive hold and raise those bloody hands. "He was hanging on to the metal edge of the seat," the policeman explained, after feeling around down there, "and it's kind of sharp." Two more policemen had come up by now and were helping him lift the man out.

"Take him around this side of the house and in the back door," Hopkins ordered with the air of a man who has just thought of something. "Give him a drink and get him up the back stairs to old Mr. Lindstrom's room. Keep him there till I'm ready for him."

He stood watching them take the man away—it wasn't necessary absolutely to carry him—and then observed to Murray, "I don't hold much with third-degree methods, but when, once in a life-time, a policeman gets a break like this I think he'd be a fool not to make the most of it." He walked off toward the front door, leaving Pete and Camilla beside the airplane.

She climbed up on the wing to look inside and see that she'd left everything as she wanted it. Pete let her alone, assuming that she knew what she wanted to do, though he had to stifle a protest when he saw her staring down into the after cockpit. This was plainly too much for her since she went very white and was glad to have him lift her down. She seemed pathetically young and small when you had hold of her like this.

"I don't wonder that was too much for you," he said. "I don't like the sight of blood any too well myself."

"It wasn't that," she told him. "I was looking at that belt. One of the buckles was jammed between the seat and the side. I didn't know he wasn't strapped in, Pete. I wasn't trying to kill him."

"He'd have killed you," he reminded her grimly but this didn't serve to lift the horror from her. She went on looking so wretched that he asked her presently if she didn't want to be put to bed.

"No, but I know what I do want," she told him, lighting up suddenly; "breakfast! I'm starved. I haven't eaten a bite since our horrible dinner last night with Mr. Taylor. You've had your breakfast, I suppose, but come along and watch me eat."

He steered her in through the west veranda so that she shouldn't encounter Taylor in the hall.

Sophy appeared to be, luckily, out of commission so Mrs. Rosnes, whose perturbations, if any, were purely internal, served her in silence and as soon as the food was on the table retired incuriously to her kitchen. One cup of coffee was all Camilla needed to bring her back to life. When she had drunk that she began, between bites, telling Pete about her adventure.

"I knew he must have just shot somebody from the look in his face when he came dashing out of the house, and of course it might have been you. If he'd killed you—well, then nothing more would matter. Nothing that could happen to me, I mean. But I didn't believe he had, somehow. I knew he couldn't do anything to me, once we had taken off.

"The only bad minute was when he thought I was stalling and didn't mean to take off. I had the valve shut, you see, and was running out the gas in the feed line; and he didn't know that I had to wait for it to fill up again. But as soon as we started to roll it was all right. He doesn't know anything about airplanes; he told me so yesterday. So I started climbing on about a ten-mile circle and kept right on doing it.

"He wanted me to fly him up north into some lonely part of Wisconsin, but I figured he wouldn't know how much altitude I'd want before I started out. When I guessed I had about seven thousand feet I stalled the ship and kicked it into its first spin. I heard him give a yell as the nose came down, and I felt pretty sure, then, that I'd be all right and that I could get him too sick and scared, before we landed, to hold the gun.

"I did everything I could think of, coming down: spins and loops, snap rolls and one upside-down glide, and a sort of home-made Immelmann. And all that time, Pete, he had nothing but his hands to hold him in with. I suppose he was so busy holding his gun on me when we started that he never thought of fastening the belt and then the buckle jiggled down and got jammed so he couldn't. Or perhaps he didn't even know what the belt was for."

She was going white again. Apparently this thing touched her professional honor; the idea of killing a passenger, even one waiting his chance to kill you, by stunting him out of your plane had the horror of nightmare in it for her. She shook her head to dismiss it and finished the subject with a pale gleam of humor. "I wouldn't have tried to kill any one like that, Pete; let alone my own brother."

Well, she might as well know it now as later—and it would give her something else to think about. "He isn't your brother," Murray told her. "He's Emil."

Chapter XII

CONFESSIONS

SHE wasn't as astounded as he'd expected her to be: when she spoke he saw why. "Where's Eric, then?" she asked. "Was it Eric he'd just shot?"

Pete was beginning to doubt the wisdom of having started this but having started he couldn't stop. "According to Hopkins," he said, "Eric *has* been shot—well, murdered, anyhow—but not this morning, and not here. Perhaps on the train. It was Emil who got off the train, at all events; Emil whom we met and had breakfast with and insisted on bringing out to identify poor Lucretia without giving him time to change his clothes."

She was staring at him incredulously and when he'd finished speaking she said, in effect, what he had said to Hopkins, "Pete, you're crazy!"

"I thought I was," he admitted, "when I began to see what Hopkins meant. The Chief doesn't pretend to know all about it but he says he's got three hard facts to go on, and I'm sure that's one of them."

"But it simply isn't possible that we could have been

fooled like that," she protested. "How many times in the last two days have we said how exactly like Eric something was that he'd just said or done; how we'd have expected him to change more than that? He even made the same jokes he used to make about grandfather. Pete, he remembered the picture post-card he'd sent me from Norway: the one with the goat on the roof."

"Emil might have remembered that just as well," said Murray, "if he was traveling with him that summer." He said it rather absently, though; the light was beginning to break over him. "Look here, Camilla! Start with the assumption that the story he told us night before last at dinner was exactly true—the meeting in the Métro; the talk in the café; the trip to Norway, and the winter in Paris afterward—all true, except that it was Emil telling it from Eric's point of view. He slipped once or twice into Emil's point of view, now that I think back. Do you remember how much stress he laid on Emil's not being interested in the relationship; how careful he was, you see, not to put Eric on his guard? And how he said that if Emil had proposed going to Norway with him, he, Eric, would certainly have declined? That was pure swank, Camilla—vanity. He couldn't help dwelling on how clever he'd been. His picture of Eric was true, too;

indiscreet, reckless, irresponsible: truer than any description Eric could have given of himself."

Camilla was only half convinced. "Emil couldn't talk any English," she objected. "He couldn't have learned to talk it as well as that in two years. I suppose he might have pretended he couldn't talk English but what would have been the sense to that?"

"Plenty of sense," Murray retorted. "That would have been the smartest thing he could do; nothing else would have gone so far to put Eric off his guard. He'd have left his letters and business papers lying around; he'd have said things in English in Emil's presence that he wouldn't have said if he thought he could understand. Think it through, Camilla! Think what a perfectly unparalleled chance it offered for an impersonation: to live with a man for the better part of a year as his courier and valet. There wasn't a trick of speech or a habit of body that could escape a scrutiny like that. Really, if we'd been a little more intelligent we might have guessed that it was an impersonation just because it was so good."

"I haven't the brains," said Camilla, "for—what do you call them?—paradoxes this morning. Come down to words of one syllable if you want me to see what you mean."

"Do you remember what you said to Hopkins in the undertaking parlor while we were waiting for Eric to identify Lucretia? Hopkins asked you if he looked natural and you said that everything he said and did made you think how exactly like Eric that was. Well, that ought to have suggested an impersonation to anybody with brains; maybe it did to Hopkins."

"Then you mean," said Camilla, "that Emil had meant, all along, to pretend he was Eric, when he got a chance, and that he had spent all that year watching him, learning his tricks and jokes and practising the high spots, like an actor?"

He nodded, but rather dubiously. "Oh, it's all right as far as it goes," he said, "but even with that allowance it still seems pretty incredible. You'd think he'd have given himself away somewhere."

"Well, he did, when you look back," Camilla suddenly declared. "Do you remember how queer he was after the funeral when old people like the Cunninghams and the Bells came up to speak to him; hardly saying a word even after we'd reminded him who they were, and acting like somebody walking in his sleep? That's more or less how you're supposed to act at a funeral, so he got away with it.—And then, Sunday dinner! He hadn't forgotten it was Sunday, Pete. He had the Sunday paper right in his hand. Eric used to *loathe* Sunday dinner and make a perfectly silly fuss about it. But *he* had to wait till I told him what time Sunday dinner was.

"Pete, I hope it's true that he isn't Eric at all. Ever since the second time he kissed me, there on the station platform—the first time was all right—I've hated him so that it almost made me sick; most of all when he was trying to be nice to me. The only thing I liked about him was the way he treated the Nelsons, after Ruth and her mother had made that scene about him, you know. Why was he so nice to them, do you suppose? Why didn't he have one of his tantrums then, the way he did when I asked him about Lucretia?"

"He must have foreseen that they'd identify him," Murray reflected, "and he wanted to get it over with while we were standing by to see how well he took it. He probably wore a cap on purpose and took pains that little Ruth should get her first glimpse of him looking at her over a bush, so that there shouldn't be any doubt about it."

He saw her go rather white as the implication behind his words broke over her but she didn't try to evade it. "He was the man, then, who came here that night to murder Lucretia. Pete, how long has he been impersonating Eric? Was it really Emil that married Lucretia? Or was the night he murdered her the first time he'd ever seen her?"

Pete shook his head and admitted that this took him beyond his depth. "I don't believe, though, that the impersonation had gone on very long when we met him at the train. Hopkins told us, before dinner Saturday night, that he was certain Eric got on the train at Los Angeles and was riding in it at the time his grandfather was murdered. I don't know whether he'd say that now or not. If he still says so it means that Eric was murdered on the train."

He saw a curious expression go across her face, a twinge of pain he took it for, and exclaimed in consternation, "I was a brute to have said that."

She shook her head. "It wasn't that," she told him. "I don't seem to have any feelings left. I guess I never did have the right sort, exactly. That's what I was grinning about.—How long is it, Pete, since we were having breakfast together in your flat, after my night out, you know?"

"That was Thursday," he calculated. "This is Monday. Four days! Good Lord!"

"Do you remember what I said when you told me Eric was coming home. I said you were all the relatives I needed. Like the mate of the Nancy brig. Well, you're all I've got, now, and you aren't a relative at all."

They heard a car in the drive start up and roll away. Her muscles tightened at the sound and then slowly relaxed. There was nothing to be afraid of any more. "I suppose that's Mr. Hopkins taking Eric to jail—Emil, I mean. So that's the end of it. You probably want to be getting off, too; back to your office. It isn't too late to start a day's work, is it? Only a little after nine?"

She might have been teasing him but her face with those big forlorn eyes didn't look like that.

"I'm not going back to the office for a while. There's something here that I've got to settle first."

It hadn't been Hopkins going away. He was standing now in the dining-room doorway looking across into the breakfast alcove where they sat. Camilla's eyes weren't looking forlorn any more and the color was back in her cheeks. "Come in!" she called to him. "You look tired and hungry. Have you had any breakfast this morning?"

"I remember drinking a cup of coffee, standing up, at some time or other since daylight," he answered, but he came in very readily and submitted without protest to having some ham and eggs ordered for him. He might be tired but he looked triumphant.

"I wish there were something adequate I could do for you," he told Camilla, "—like giving you a special gold medal, to show my appreciation of what you've done in this case. I suppose you'd be best pleased, both of you, if I kept your share of it dark and swallowed all the credit myself."

"You mean you've got the confession you wanted?" Murray guessed.

The Chief nodded. "A pair of them. Taylor sang his song first. He thought Emil had double-crossed him. And Emil, in the state his airplane ride and a couple of drinks had left him, told everything he knew. He talked so fast that Samuels, the stenographer, could hardly keep up with him. He didn't want to do anything *but* talk; not even stop for breath. I think I know the whole thing, now.—There's one loose end," he added, turning to Murray, "that I'm going to have to ask you to help me tie, but that's only a formality, really. So in a day or two, when you've had a chance to get rested,"—this to Camilla—"I'll come around and tell you the whole story."

"And you've been so *intelligent* up to that very last sentence!" she exclaimed. "Do you think I'm going to wait two days? Or two hours? Can't you go on sitting right there in that chair, and have some more coffee, and tell it now?"

The Chief grinned. "That's what I hoped you'd want me to do," he admitted. "Here goes, then. I won't make it any longer than I can help.

"The man you took for a ride this morning in your airplane is a well-known international crook known to his profession as English Ed. He gets that nickname not because he's English, for he isn't, but because of his success in impersonating Englishmen, particularly aristocratic or titled Englishmen. He has a string of aliases as long as your arm, but his real name, queerly enough, is Emil Lindstrom. I got that clue out of the family Bible and confirmed it by cable last night. He's the typical black sheep or bad egg of a good family— he really is a distant cousin of yours—and he's got a police record here and all over Europe that's at least ten years old. He's got two notable weaknesses: he's an inveterate gambler—which many of them are—but the other's more unusual; he's yellow, and on that account not as highly regarded in his profession as he would be on his talents, which are brilliant and varied. He can do more different things well than most successful criminals. I owe this biography mostly to Taylor.

"Well, then, we start in Paris. You can take the story Emil told us at dinner Saturday night as substantially true, with the necessary adjustments, of course. He got on Eric's trail and saw the chance the resemblance between them afforded for a really brilliant stroke. He spent months with Eric learning all he could about him, learning to write his handwriting, practising every detail for a successful impersonation. I don't know just what his plan was. It doesn't matter, for he got no chance at that time to carry it out. Somehow or other Eric's marriage with Lucrèce Pasteur spoiled it.

"She was sort of a cosmopolitan herself, with an English mother and a French father, living in Paris by her wits when she landed Eric. She wasn't a crook exactly, certainly not from Emil's point of view, but she was pretty hard-boiled and she took some precautions that made Emil's game difficult to play. They heard about each other but never met. Emil saw her once but took pains that she shouldn't see him. He filed his data about Eric for future reference in that extraordinary brain of his and began hunting other game.

"He got into this country on a forged passport about a year ago, and presently hooked up with the man you know as Gordon Taylor. He's a professional crook too, with a string of aliases of his own. They made a successful team and got on very well together until a couple of months ago when Emil's crooked streak got the better of him—crooked from the crook's point of view, I mean—and he ran out on Taylor with the whole proceeds of a successful haul; left Taylor holding the bag.

"Emil came out here to Chicago and lost the whole amount playing the races. This put him in a very bad position indeed, for Taylor tracked him out here. Taylor isn't very formidable personally but he's got some dangerous gang connections and he served notice on Emil that unless he repaid the money within a week he'd be bumped off. That was last Wednesday.

"In his desperation Emil decided to come out here. He had two chances. The best chance, and the most congenial to his talents, was Eric himself. If Eric were at home, and he thought he might be, there was a chance for temporary shelter and for copious blackmail. He had various things on Eric, chiefly his secret marriage. If Eric weren't at home there was the safe in the study."

Camilla and Murray both exclaimed over that.

"Yes," the Chief admitted, "it's queer, but no queerer

than lots of things that men babble to strangers about. Eric liked to make fun of his grandfather and tell stories about his queer ways. And one of these stories was the twenty-five thousand dollars—'the Chicago fire money,' he called it—that was kept lying idle in the safe under the study stairs waiting for some other catastrophe—perhaps an earthquake. Emil wasn't a yegg—that means a criminal who drills safes and blows them open with nitroglycerine—but he could open them sometimes, especially the old ones, by sound and feel.

"Well, he came to the gate that evening and asked for Eric, just as Mrs. Nelson testified at the inquest; he hung about and saw her and her husband go away. As you know, he stole into the grounds while little Ruth was across the road buying her candy bars. He didn't mean to try to get into the house until late that night after the family had retired, but the partly open study window and the sight of you people at dinner tempted him to steal in for a preliminary look. He saw Eric's telegram lying on the desk and read it. That was what he was doing when Lucretia surprised him.

"She mistook him for Eric; called him Eric, but in a whisper. She must have had the idea that he'd flown to Chicago ahead of his train. He silenced her by putting his finger to his lips, and this must have convinced her that he'd come on to see her secretly. Emil didn't know what her position in the household was nor what her relations with Eric were, but he was quick-witted enough to take full advantage of her mistake. She conducted him without a word up the private stair-case through Mr. Lindstrom's room and across to her own.

"She puzzled him by saying as she left him that it wouldn't do him any good to search her room because the thing he wanted to find wasn't there. It's clear to me in the light of what Emil found out later that she referred to her marriage certificate, which was of course locked up in the safe. What Emil did search her room for was a letter, or a packet of letters, from Eric. He hoped that they would give him some facts which would enable him to stave off detection for a few hours at least so that he could stay safely hidden in the house until the family had gone to bed and he could get at the safe.

"He didn't find any letters and he began to get uneasy lest Lucretia, who evidently wasn't on any too friendly terms with Eric, might betray him. So he crossed over into old Mr. Lindstrom's room as a matter of strategic precaution. If he heard her bringing people up the main staircase he could escape by the little one. While he waited for her he searched Mr. Lindstrom's room—on general principles. Almost anything might be fish that came to his net.

"He did find your target pistol and was glad to have it. He never carried any weapon himself but a small blackjack. He had no idea at that time, he says, of shooting anybody. He wanted the gun for a bluff to silence Lucretia with. He heard her come up the stairs alone and a moment later heard you and Mr. Lindstrom go into the study. His eye fell on the speaking-tube and he opened the cap. This was a real find, since he began almost at once hearing the, to him, vitally important conversation that was going on in the room below."

"It certainly was important," Murray agreed, and, for Camilla's benefit, summarized it: "How to work the secret drawer, the fact that he kept the combination to the safe in it, his suspicion that Lucretia had memorized it with the intention of stealing the money, and his intention to dismiss her. You could call that an earful, all right. But what was Lucretia doing all this time?"

"She came in almost at once, having merely gone to her room first and found that he wasn't there. He motioned to her to shut the door and come and listen, which her curiosity led her to do without making a sound. Neither of them moved until the conversation came to an end. He noticed, though, that she was looking at him pretty intently and suspected her of beginning to doubt his being Eric. The white cotton gloves he was wearing may have had a good deal to do with it but there's another possibility which he didn't see. If he'd really been Eric his grandfather's determination to dismiss Lucretia would have meant more to him than it did. You'll see why, presently. Anyhow, as he straightened up from the tube but before he released the cap, his coat swung open and she saw the pistol. That was enough to make her scream.

"It was only in surprise, however; she hadn't yet made up her mind to give him away. She declared she didn't believe he was Eric, and on his still insisting that he was, asked him some questions he couldn't answer. He saw she'd identified him, all right, but she wasted a few minutes trying to find out what his game was, possibly playing with the idea that there might be a part in it for her. Presently she made up her mind, however, and darted for the door, the door into the upper hall. He beat her to it by a step, turned the key in the lock, and to keep her from screaming again, pulled out the pistol. He says he didn't suppose it was loaded, but of course it was and it went off right in her face.

"I think he must have completely lost his nerve for a minute, for he isn't a natural born killer. He says that what rattled him was the sound of an automobile engine starting up just at the instant the shot went off. That must have been you, taking Mrs. Smith down to the gate. Anyhow, he stood there paralyzed until he heard Mr. Lindstrom coming up the private staircase. He shot him from the top of the stairs. He stood listening a few seconds; the automobile rolled away; the house was dead still.

"We already knew what he did after that: how he got the combination out of the drawer, unlocked the safe, got Mr. Lindstrom's keys out of his pocket to unlock the inner compartment; took the money; locked up the safe; carried the gun up-stairs and laid it beside Lucretia, but forgetting to press her hand against the butt. The only thing we hadn't figured out was the thing that led directly to his next crime—Eric's telegram on the desk. Without knowing exactly why, he says, he stuck that in his pocket and carried it away with him. He escaped from the house and the grounds just as we calculated that he must have done.

"Well, the story might have ended there just as well as not. Except for a bit of what he regarded at the time as bad luck it would have. He closed the gate behind him and was about to lock it when an automobile pulled into the filling station across the road at such an angle that its bright headlights were turned full on the gates. He jumped aside just before the glare caught him into a recess that was in black shadow, safe enough but practically imprisoned there until the car should have filled up and driven away.

"While he waited, furious at being trapped like that, Nelson brought out the Rolls-Royce, Mrs. Smith's luggage was packed into it and the fact that she was taking her train at Oak Park for Salt Lake City made plain to the man in the shadow. The idea that that would be a good train for him to take, too, occurred to him simply because it offered the quickest way of getting as far as possible from the scene of his crime. The other possibility didn't occur to him till later.

"He started walking along the highway, got two or three short lifts, and finally took a taxicab to the Oak Park station. Outside of the loot from the safe he had very little money, less than ten dollars. And the stolen currency embarrassed him, not only because it was all of it in hundreds and fifties, but because of the large size of the bills themselves. They're rather noticeable now. There was no help for it, though, and he used one of the hundred-dollar bills at the Oak Park station to buy a coach ticket to Omaha.

"When the train came in he climbed into the smoker, where most of the passengers were already asleep. He'd picked up a time-table in the station out of mere idle curiosity. But as he studied it in the train he was suddenly struck by a coincidence and he pulled out Eric's telegram for comparison.—Well, I don't wonder it looked like fate to him. I'm not superstitious but I guess I'd have taken it the same way.

"The fact staring him in the face was that this train of his was going out to meet Eric's train. His train, the *Continental Limited,* was going to reach Cheyenne, Wyoming, at one-twenty-five to-morrow night. Eric's train, also the *Continental Limited,* eastbound, would reach Cheyenne in the dead of the same night, a little less than three hours later. And Eric's telegram, by way of a hint to Lucretia that she could telegraph to him, told the name of his car and even the number of his drawing-room. The chance this offered was, of course, absolutely dazzling; terrifying, too; not in that it involved a third murder but in that it offered an apparently perfect security from detection in the earlier two.

"He never doubted his ability to impersonate Eric successfully even in more critical circumstances than

[298]

these would be. Eric was going to people who hadn't seen him for more than eight years. The Eric who got off that train in Chicago would be able to satisfy any doubts they might have of his identity in three minutes—and why should they have any doubts at all? Given a decent break in the luck and a firm command of his nerves during a rather nasty quarter of an hour and he could step for life into the shoes of a millionaire!

"Well, he spent the rest of the night thinking about it but he'd come to his decision at the end of the first minute. The luck broke his way so consistently that it worried him a little. When the eastbound train pulled into the yards at Cheyenne and they began cutting it and switching it about, the car, Carborundum, was left as the bare end of half the train. It was no trick at all to swarm over the bumpers and the gate. He had a simple pick-lock in his pocket, a slightly perverted button-hook, but he didn't even need to use it for Eric hadn't taken the precaution to lock the door of his drawing-room.

"He roused a little when Emil opened the door but not enough to cry out before the black-jack came down hard on his head. Emil then locked the door, stripped the body of its pajamas and dressed it from skin out in the soiled and tumbled clothes he himself had been wearing since the day before he had committed the double murder here. There was one trifling embarrassment in this connection but he didn't see that it mattered much. When the train was under way again and a few miles east of Cheyenne he opened the window wide and thrust the body out upon the right-of-way. Then he shut the window, dressed himself in the dead man's pajamas and lay down on his bed to wait for morning. He admits he didn't sleep much.

"He had the whole of the next day, you'll notice, to himself—last Friday, that was—to get himself together, plan his campaign, and what was most important, to study the contents of Eric's hand luggage. He'd have liked to go into the baggage car and look through Eric's trunks too but thought he'd better not risk it. What occupied most of his time in the drawing-room was a brief-case containing, among other things, a letter of credit, which provided him pretty well with Eric's itinerary in the Far East, and a letter from Lucretia which gave a line on his motive for coming home.

"This had been written months before and had followed him from point to point half-way around the world. Apparently he'd got tired of her and deserted her very soon after their marriage. The letter served notice on him that she'd got herself into a very strong strategic position as his grandfather's private secretary. She was in high favor, she said, and could do practically anything she liked. But if Eric would be a good boy and come home and acknowledge her as his wife, she'd square him, with his grandfather.

"Well, there isn't much more that you need to be told. It fitted in badly with his plans to have you two meet him at the train but he got out of that all right, he thought. He got a nasty shock in the village just as you were driving up to the undertaking establishment when he caught a glimpse of Taylor but he rather thought Taylor hadn't seen him. He was undeceived that evening when Taylor telephoned him.

"Taylor wasn't dead sure, though, of his identification. The papers had carried Eric's picture in connection with their first story of the crime and Taylor had gone out to Oak Ridge in the hope of getting a look at him. In order to make sure, he wanted to confront the supposed Eric when they were alone and talk to him. He accomplished this Sunday morning by wading the river. Emil tried at first to bluff him out but couldn't get away with it. Taylor pointed out that they'd both been finger-printed and challenged him to go down to the bureau of identification.

[301]

"At that Emil caved in and, with one suppression, admitted the whole thing. It was practically making Taylor a partner for life, of course, in an enterprise that would run into millions. Taylor naturally agreed to the bargain. He was to help Emil every way he could; run any awkward errands for him, and so on.

"But Taylor wanted money—a lot of money—at once and Emil protested that he hadn't any. He'd surpressed the fact that he'd taken twenty-five thousand dollars from the safe. He wanted that at hand, you see, where he could grab it and stuff it into his pocket if anything unexpected happened and he found he had to bolt. Taylor, in spite of his protests, suspected that this was the case.

"This money was a real embarrassment to Emil; it was too bulky to carry easily on his person; he tried hiding it in a corner of Eric's dark room but abandoned that place for various reasons. For one thing, if he had to leave suddenly he might not even have time to go up to the third floor; for another, he suspected Carl of being a cop and his own living quarters of being especially liable to search. If the money were found there it would directly incriminate him.

"The hiding-place he finally hit upon was behind some of the books in the bookcase in the study. That wasn't very secure but it had quite a lot of compensating advantages. The room had already been thoroughly searched since the night of the crime; a man in a hurry could get it in a very few seconds and bolt, either by the door or by one of the windows; and last of all, if the money were found there its presence wouldn't necessarily incriminate him.

"You remember, of course, what happened last night in the study when he stumbled over one of the very books the money lay hidden behind. He gave himself away then to Taylor, who was taking it all in, and of course he knew it. Taylor went down into the study as soon as the house had quieted down for the night and found the three packages of bills with no trouble at all. Emil, who'd suspected this was what he would do, surprised him there but there was nothing he could do about it. He meant to kill Taylor as soon as he could get a decent chance to do so, but the situation simply wouldn't bear another murder on the premises.

"They quarreled venomously for an hour there in the study, but it couldn't go beyond words and low voices. Carl was listening to it as well as he could through the speaking-tube in Mr. Lindstrom's room but he was under my orders not to start anything and not to act at all except in a real emergency. I wanted to wait until Taylor was actually leaving and I could catch him with the goods.

"Well, there you are! Lord, how I've been talking! May I have another cup of coffee, Miss Camilla?"

"Don't give it to him!" Murray cried excitedly. "He's holding out on us. He hasn't told us the most important thing of all. The shoes, man! What the devil had the shoes to do with it?"

Hopkins grinned. "Well, I was saving that up," he admitted, "out of pure vanity. I am proud of it. It's the best piece of detective work I've ever done. Give me the coffee and I'll tell you.

"Do you remember," he asked Murray, "the imprint of a rubber heel on the back of the slip of paper that had the combination written on it? You made the remark that it must have been kicking around the study all the morning under foot. I felt rather cheap about that and of course I satisfied myself within an hour that no heel worn by anybody who'd been in that room since Nelson forced the door could have made that print. I managed to see yours when I had you kneel down in front of the safe. Old Mr. Lindstrom the night before had been wearing his house slippers. So the print was the print of the murderer's heel.

"Well, on Saturday morning when you two drove

Eric, as you supposed, out to the undertaker's establishment Nelson couldn't get the car up to the curb and you had to walk in the street, which had just been oiled. The linoleum floor was badly tracked up, and among the tracks I saw a heel that looked familiar.

"I made sure that the linoleum in the morgue itself was clean, and then I sent Eric, as we called him, in there alone to make the identification. And he left the prettiest prints you ever saw across that floor! I had the best of them photographed and enlarged, as I had already had the other, within an hour of the time he left to drive back to town. There was absolutely no doubt of the identity of the heel that made the two prints. The latter one showed a little more wear and a few new scars, but all the old ones were there and unmistakable. Whoever Eric might be, the shoe on his foot had been in the study the night of the murder.

"That was startling enough by itself, and it was still more so when I got my reports from the train crew that the same passenger had made the entire trip from Los Angeles to Chicago in that drawing-room. I wasted a little while playing with the idea of an airplane, and then I came down to earth and studied railway time-tables. If the murderer had caught Mrs.

Smith's train he could have met Eric's train in the middle of the night at Cheyenne.

"He might of course simply have handed Eric the shoes and let him wear them back, but that didn't make sense. But Mrs. Nelson's identification and little Ruth's when you told me about it before dinner Saturday night, pretty nearly did make sense. A man who looked as much like Eric as that could have taken his place on the train, though he could hardly have persuaded Eric Lindstrom to acquiesce in such a change except by killing him first.

"But here was the question that made me sweat. Assuming that the murderer, Emil, did kill Eric and dress him in his clothes and push him out of the window, why didn't he change shoes with him too? He'd have suffered a lot of inconvenience and discomfort in order not to wear back to Chicago the shoes which had been on the scene of the murder and might have left tracks. The only explanation I could see was that there must have been something about Eric's shoes that made it physically impossible for Emil to put them on his feet. Emil had been his valet; it was probable that he'd worn Eric's shoes often enough in Paris; or if he hadn't been able to he'd have remembered the fact. And this pointed to some sort of accident to one of Eric's feet since the two men had parted.

"It was a long shot but I played it. Saturday night after I left you here I called up the Chief of Police at Cheyenne on the telephone and asked him to find out whether the body of a shabbily dressed man had been found within the last thirty-six hours on or near the railroad track anywhere within twenty miles east of Cheyenne, and whether there was anything queer about either of his feet. Yesterday the Chief telegraphed me that such a body had been found and that one of the big toes had been amputated, the shoe containing a built-in support apparently to assist in walking. Both shoes showed less wear and were of better quality than the rest of the clothes.

"I figured that Eric must have possessed a lot of shoes to go with the rest of his wardrobe and that the presence of these shoes, which he couldn't possibly wear, must be an acute embarrassment to Emil. They'd be infernally hard to dispose of. When I heard about all the luggage that Taylor was bringing with him for a mere overnight stay, and when Carl reported that none of the bags were packed anywhere near full, I made up my mind that this was the real purpose of Taylor's visit.

That was another long shot that worked.

"Well, there are the three hard facts I had."

"The identity of the heel-print," said Murray; "the

body with the amputated big toe. Those are two of them. What is the third?"

"Oh, yes," said Hopkins. "The third was the set of finger-prints that Carl collected from the dinner table last night. They found them at the identification bureau, without any trouble—English Ed and Gordon Taylor. That made enough to justify an arrest, all right. But Lord, how those confessions helped!"

He'd finished his coffee and lighted his pipe. "I must be in something the same frame of mind as Emil," he remarked. "I've been for a ride and I wanted to talk. I guess I'd better go back and resume my duties as Chief of Police; especially as I've got to go out to Cheyenne to-night. That's the thing I wanted of you," he went on, turning to Murray. "Will you go with me to make the identification, or is there any one else who can do it better?"

"Not that I can think of," said Murray. "I'll be glad to go, of course."

Camilla was looking very thoughtful. "It was the real Eric wasn't it, that we telegraphed to," she asked, "saying that grandfather and Lucretia had been murdered? Well, and it must have been the real Eric who telegraphed back that he was desolated but not to delay the funeral for him." You could read in her face the thought that her own brother hadn't shown much more human feeling than his murderer.

But Murray thought of something else. "How did Emil know about that telegram?" he asked. "He did, all right. He spoke of it."

"I forgot to mention that," said Hopkins, "—and Emil rather dwelt on it, too, as part of his good luck. The pad Eric had written the telegram on was still in the drawing-room and the impressions of the pencil were legible on the next sheet." He got up with a sigh. "I hope you people never get mixed up in any more murders," he said, "but it's a very unselfish wish. Because I don't suppose I shall ever find anybody else as friendly and as intelligent to work with."

They went out into the veranda with him and watched him drive away with Walsh in his side-car.

"Well, that's the end of it," said Camilla. "And now you can go back to Miss Foster at the office and forget your troubles. I'll probably drop in for a minute this afternoon and say good-by. I'm going to telegraph the Fairchild Murrays at Eastpoint, I think, and tell them I'm coming down for the rest of the summer. They asked me to, you know, when they were trying to get me to say I'd go to that school in Florence next winter with Eunice. And Eunice wrote again just last week. I may as well get off to-day if they wire that it's all right. I can get my tickets without any trouble, and I've plenty of money.—What's the matter with that plan, Pete? I'm not wanted here for anything, am I?"

She'd made that long speech rather fast and almost to the end without looking at him. He'd been looking at her all the time but the voice he'd wanted to interrupt her with had simply refused to work at all. It was still frozen now that she had fallen silent upon a direct question. He went right on looking at her but he couldn't say a word; all he could do was to reach out for her with his hands.

She stepped back away from him. "Not unless you mean it, Pete," she said. "I couldn't stand it."

Apparently, though, she saw he did mean it, for, the next instant, with a gasp, she flung herself upon him.

THE END

THE PERENNIAL LIBRARY MYSTERY SERIES

E. C. Bentley

TRENT'S LAST CASE
"One of the three best detective stories ever written."

—Agatha Christie

TRENT'S OWN CASE
"I won't waste time saying that the plot is sound and the detection satisfying. Trent has not altered a scrap and reappears with all his old humor and charm." —Dorothy L. Sayers

Gavin Black

A DRAGON FOR CHRISTMAS
"Potent excitement!" —New York Herald Tribune

THE EYES AROUND ME
"I stayed up until all hours last night reading *The Eyes Around Me*, which is something I do not do very often, but I was so intrigued by the ingeniousness of Mr. Black's plotting and the witty way in which he spins his mystery. I can only say that I enjoyed the book enormously."

—F. van Wyck Mason

YOU WANT TO DIE, JOHNNY?
"Gavin Black doesn't just develop a pressure plot in suspense, he adds uninfected wit, character, charm, and sharp knowledge of the Far East to make rereading as keen as the first race-through." —Book Week

Nicholas Blake

THE BEAST MUST DIE
"It remains one more proof that in the hands of a really first-class writer the detective novel can safely challenge comparison with any other variety of fiction." —The Manchester Guardian

THE CORPSE IN THE SNOWMAN
"If there is a distinction between the novel and the detective story (which we do not admit), then this book deserves a high place in both categories." —The New York Times

THE DREADFUL HOLLOW
"Pace unhurried, characters excellent, reasoning solid."

—San Francisco Chronicle

END OF CHAPTER
". . . admirably solid . . . an adroit formal detective puzzle backed up by firm characterization and a knowing picture of London publishing."
—*The New York Times*

HEAD OF A TRAVELER
"Another grade A detective story of the right old jigsaw persuasion."
—*New York Herald Tribune Book Review*

MINUTE FOR MURDER
"An outstanding mystery novel. Mr. Blake's writing is a delight in itself."
—*The New York Times*

THE MORNING AFTER DEATH
"One of Blake's best."
—Rex Warner

A PENKNIFE IN MY HEART
"Style brilliant . . . and suspenseful."
—*San Francisco Chronicle*

THE PRIVATE WOUND
[Blake's] best novel in a dozen years . . . . An intensely penetrating study of sexual passion . . . . A powerful story of murder and its aftermath."
—Anthony Boucher, *The New York Times*

A QUESTION OF PROOF
"The characters in this story are unusually well drawn, and the suspense is well sustained."
—*The New York Times*

THE SAD VARIETY
"It is a stunner. I read it instead of eating, instead of sleeping."
—Dorothy Salisbury Davis

THE SMILER WITH THE KNIFE
"An extraordinarily well written and entertaining thriller."
—*Saturday Review of Literature*

THOU SHELL OF DEATH
"It has all the virtues of culture, intelligence and sensibility that the most exacting connoisseur could ask of detective fiction."
—*The Times* [London] *Literary Supplement*

THE WHISPER IN THE GLOOM
"One of the most entertaining suspense-pursuit novels in many seasons."
—*The New York Times*

Nicolas Blake (cont'd)

THE WIDOW'S CRUISE

"A stirring suspense. . . . The thrilling tale leaves nothing to be desired."
—*Springfield Republican*

THE WORM OF DEATH

"It [The Worm of Death] is one of Blake's very best—and his best is better than almost anyone's." —Louis Untermeyer

George Harmon Coxe

MURDER WITH PICTURES

"[Coxe] has hit the bull's-eye with his first shot."
—*The New York Times*

Edmund Crispin

BURIED FOR PLEASURE

"Absolute and unalloyed delight."
—Anthony Boucher, *The New York Times*

Kenneth Fearing

THE BIG CLOCK

"It will be some time before chill-hungry clients meet again so rare a compound of irony, satire, and icy-fingered narrative. *The Big Clock* is . . . a psychothriller you won't put down." —*Weekly Book Review*

Andrew Garve

THE ASHES OF LODA

"Garve . . . embellishes a fine fast adventure story with a more credible picture of the U.S.S.R. than is offered in most thrillers."
—*The New York Times Book Review*

THE CUCKOO LINE AFFAIR

". . . an agreeable and ingenious piece of work." —*The New Yorker*

A HERO FOR LEANDA

"One can trust Mr. Garve to put a fresh twist to any situation, and the ending is really a lovely surprise." —*The Manchester Guardian*

MURDER THROUGH THE LOOKING GLASS

". . . refreshingly out-of-the-way and enjoyable . . . highly recommended to all comers." —*Saturday Review*

Andrew Garve (cont'd)

NO TEARS FOR HILDA

"It starts fine and finishes finer. I got behind on breathing watching Max get not only his man but his woman, too." —Rex Stout

THE RIDDLE OF SAMSON

"The story is an excellent one, the people are quite likable, and the writing is superior." —*Springfield Republican*

Michael Gilbert

BLOOD AND JUDGMENT

"Gilbert readers need scarcely be told that the characters all come alive at first sight, and that his surpassing talent for narration enhances any plot. . . . Don't miss." —*San Francisco Chronicle*

THE BODY OF A GIRL

"Does what a good mystery should do: open up into all kinds of ramifications, with untold menace behind the action. At the end, there is a bang-up climax, and it is a pleasure to see how skilfully Gilbert wraps everything up." —*The New York Times Book Review*

THE DANGER WITHIN

"Michael Gilbert has nicely combined some elements of the straight detective story with plenty of action, suspense, and adventure, to produce a superior thriller." —*Saturday Review*

DEATH HAS DEEP ROOTS

"Trial scenes superb; prowl along Loire vivid chase stuff; funny in right places; a fine performance throughout." —*Saturday Review*

FEAR TO TREAD

"Merits serious consideration as a work of art."
—*The New York Times*

C. W. Grafton

BEYOND A REASONABLE DOUBT

"A very ingenious tale of murder . . . a brilliant and gripping narrative."
—Jacques Barzun and Wendell Hertig Taylor

Edward Grierson

THE SECOND MAN

"One of the best trial-testimony books to have come along in quite a while." —*The New Yorker*

Cyril Hare

AN ENGLISH MURDER
"By a long shot, the best crime story I have read for a long time. Everything is traditional, but originality does not suffer. The setting is perfect. Full marks to Mr. Hare." —*Irish Press*

TRAGEDY AT LAW
"An extremely urbane and well-written detective story."
—*The New York Times*

UNTIMELY DEATH
"The English detective story at its quiet best, meticulously underplayed, rich in perceivings of the droll human animal and ready at the last with a neat surprise which has been there all the while had we but wits to see it." —*New York Herald Tribune Book Review*

WHEN THE WIND BLOWS
"The best, unquestionably, of all the Hare stories, and a masterpiece by any standards."
—Jacques Barzun and Wendell Hertig Taylor, *A Catalogue of Crime*

WITH A BARE BODKIN
"One of the best detective stories published for a long time."
—*The Spectator*

Matthew Head

THE CABINDA AFFAIR (*available 6/81*)
"An absorbing whodunit and a distinguished novel of atmosphere."
—Anthony Boucher, *The New York Times*

MURDER AT THE FLEA CLUB (*available 6/81*)
"The true delight is in Head's style, its limpid ease combined with humor and an awesome precision of phrase." —*San Francisco Chronicle*

M. V. Heberden

ENGAGED TO MURDER
"Smooth plotting." —*The New York Times*

James Hilton

WAS IT MURDER?
"The story is well planned and well written."
—*The New York Times*

Elspeth Huxley

THE AFRICAN POISON MURDERS
"Obscure venom, manical mutilations, deadly bush fire, thrilling climax compose major opus.... Top-flight."
—*Saturday Review of Literature*

Francis Iles

BEFORE THE FACT
"Not many 'serious' novelists have produced character studies to compare with Iles's internally terrifying portrait of the murderer in *Before the Fact,* his masterpiece and a work truly deserving the appellation of unique and beyond price." —Howard Haycraft

MALICE AFORETHOUGHT
"It is a long time since I have read anything so good as *Malice Aforethought,* with its cynical humour, acute criminology, plausible detail and rapid movement. It makes you hug yourself with pleasure."
—H. C. Harwood, *Saturday Review*

Lange Lewis

THE BIRTHDAY MURDER
"Almost perfect in its playlike purity and delightful prose."
—Jacques Barzun and Wendell Hertig Taylor

Arthur Maling

LUCKY DEVIL
"The plot unravels at a fast clip, the writing is breezy and Maling's approach is as fresh as today's stockmarket quotes."
—*Louisville Courier Journal*

RIPOFF
"A swiftly paced story of today's big business is larded with intrigue as a Ralph Nader-type investigates an insurance scandal and is soon on the run from a hired gun and his brother. . . . Engrossing and credible."
—*Booklist*

SCHROEDER'S GAME
"As the title indicates, this Schroeder is up to something, and the unravelling of his game is a diverting and sufficiently blood-soaked entertainment."
—*The New Yorker*

Thomas Sterling

THE EVIL OF THE DAY

"Prose as witty and subtle as it is sharp and clear...characters unconventionally conceived and richly bodied forth . . . . In short, a novel to be treasured."　　　　　　　　—Anthony Boucher, *The New York Times*

Julian Symons

THE BELTING INHERITANCE

"A superb whodunit in the best tradition of the detective story."
　　　　　　　　—August Derleth, *Madison Capital Times*

BLAND BEGINNING

"Mr. Symons displays a deft storytelling skill, a quiet and literate wit, a nice feeling for character, and detectival ingenuity of a high order."
　　　　　　　　—Anthony Boucher, *The New York Times*

BOGUE'S FORTUNE

"There's a touch of the old sardonic humour, and more than a touch of style."　　　　　　　　　　　　　　　—*The Spectator*

THE BROKEN PENNY

"The most exciting, astonishing and believable spy story to appear in years.　　　—Anthony Boucher, *The New York Times Book Review*

THE COLOR OF MURDER

"A singularly unostentatious and memorably brilliant detective story."
　　　　　　　　—*New York Herald Tribune Book Review*

THE 31ST OF FEBRUARY

"Nobody has painted a more gruesome picture of the advertising business since Dorothy Sayers wrote 'Murder Must Advertise', and very few people have written a more entertaining or dramatic mystery story."
　　　　　　　　—*The New Yorker*

Dorothy Stockbridge Tillet
(John Stephen Strange)

THE MAN WHO KILLED FORTESCUE

"Better than average."　　　　　—*Saturday Review of Literature*

Henry Kitchell Webster

WHO IS THE NEXT?

"A double murder, private-plane piloting, a neat impersonation, and a delicate courtship are adroitly combined by a writer who knows how to use the language."　　　—Jacques Barzun and Wendell Hertig Taylor

Anna Mary Wells

MURDERER'S CHOICE
"Good writing, ample action, and excellent character work."
—*Saturday Review of Literature*

A TALENT FOR MURDER
"The discovery of the villain is a decided shock."   —*Books*

**If you enjoyed this book you'll want to know about
THE PERENNIAL LIBRARY MYSTERY SERIES**

Nicholas Blake

☐	P 456	THE BEAST MUST DIE	$1.95
☐	P 427	THE CORPSE IN THE SNOWMAN	$1.95
☐	P 493	THE DREADFUL HOLLOW	$1.95
☐	P 397	END OF CHAPTER	$1.95
☐	P 419	MINUTE FOR MURDER	$1.95
☐	P 520	THE MORNING AFTER DEATH	$1.95
☐	P 521	A PENKNIFE IN MY HEART	$2.25
☐	P 531	THE PRIVATE WOUND	$2.25
☐	P 494	A QUESTION OF PROOF	$1.95
☐	P 495	THE SAD VARIETY	$2.25
☐	P 457	THE SMILER WITH THE KNIFE	$1.95
☐	P 428	THOU SHELL OF DEATH	$1.95
☐	P 418	THE WHISPER IN THE GLOOM	$1.95
☐	P 399	THE WIDOW'S CRUISE	$1.95
☐	P 400	THE WORM OF DEATH	$2.25

E. C. Bentley

☐	P 440	TRENT'S LAST CASE	$1.95
☐	P 516	TRENT'S OWN CASE	$2.25

Buy them at your local bookstore or use this coupon for ordering:

**HARPER & ROW, Mail Order Dept. #PMS, 10 East 53rd St.,
New York, N.Y. 10022.**
Please send me the books I have checked above. I am enclosing $ _____
which includes a postage and handling charge of $1.00 for the first book and
25¢ for each additional book. Send check or money order. No cash or
C.O.D.'s please.

Name _____

Address _____

City _____ State _____ Zip _____
Please allow 4 weeks for delivery. USA and Canada only. This offer expires
2/1/82. Please add applicable sales tax.

Gavin Black

☐ P 473   A DRAGON FOR CHRISTMAS $1.95
☐ P 485   THE EYES AROUND ME $1.95
☐ P 472   YOU WANT TO DIE, JOHNNY? $1.95

George Harmon Coxe

☐ P 527   MURDER WITH PICTURES $2.25

Edmund Crispin

☐ P 506   BURIED FOR PLEASURE $1.95

Kenneth Fearing

☐ P 500   THE BIG CLOCK $1.95

Andrew Garve

☐ P 430   THE ASHES OF LODA $1.50
☐ P 451   THE CUCKOO LINE AFFAIR $1.95
☐ P 429   A HERO FOR LEANDA $1.50
☐ P 449   MURDER THROUGH THE LOOKING
           GLASS $1.95
☐ P 441   NO TEARS FOR HILDA $1.95
☐ P 450   THE RIDDLE OF SAMSON $1.95

Buy them at your local bookstore or use this coupon for ordering:

Michael Gilbert

- [ ] P 446   BLOOD AND JUDGMENT $1.95
- [ ] P 459   THE BODY OF A GIRL $1.95
- [ ] P 448   THE DANGER WITHIN $1.95
- [ ] P 447   DEATH HAS DEEP ROOTS $1.95
- [ ] P 458   FEAR TO TREAD $1.95

C. W. Grafton

- [ ] P 519   BEYOND A REASONABLE DOUBT $1.95

Edward Grierson

- [ ] P 528   THE SECOND MAN $2.25

Cyril Hare

- [ ] P 455   AN ENGLISH MURDER $1.95
- [ ] P 522   TRAGEDY AT LAW $2.25
- [ ] P 514   UNTIMELY DEATH $1.95
- [ ] P 454   WHEN THE WIND BLOWS $1.95
- [ ] P 523   WITH A BARE BODKIN $2.25

Matthew Head

- [ ] P 541   THE CABINDA AFFAIR (available 6/81) $2.25
- [ ] P 542   MURDER AT THE FLEA CLUB
  (available 6/81) $2.25

Buy them at your local bookstore or use this coupon for ordering:

HARPER & ROW, Mail Order Dept. #PMS, 10 East 53rd St., New York, N.Y. 10022.
Please send me the books I have checked above. I am enclosing $ _____ which includes a postage and handling charge of $1.00 for the first book and 25¢ for each additional book. Send check or money order. No cash or C.O.D.'s please.

Name _____

Address _____

City _____ State _____ Zip _____
Please allow 4 weeks for delivery. USA and Canada only. This offer expires 2/1/82. Please add applicable sales tax.

M. V. Heberden

☐ P 533 ENGAGED TO MURDER $2.25

James Hilton

☐ P 501 WAS IT MURDER? $1.95

Elspeth Huxley

☐ P 540 THE AFRICAN POISON MURDERS

$2.25

Frances Iles

☐ P 517 BEFORE THE FACT $1.95
☐ P 532 MALICE AFORETHOUGHT $1.95

Lange Lewis

☐ P 518 THE BIRTHDAY MURDER $1.95

Arthur Maling

☐ P 482 LUCKY DEVIL $1.95
☐ P 483 RIPOFF $1.95
☐ P 484 SCHROEDER'S GAME $1.95

Austin Ripley

☐ P 387 MINUTE MYSTERIES $1.95

Buy them at your local bookstore or use this coupon for ordering:

HARPER & ROW, Mail Order Dept. #PMS, 10 East 53rd St., New York, N.Y. 10022.

Please send me the books I have checked above. I am enclosing $ _____ which includes a postage and handling charge of $1.00 for the first book and 25¢ for each additional book. Send check or money order. No cash or C.O.D.'s please.

Name _____

Address _____

City _____ State _____ Zip _____

Please allow 4 weeks for delivery. USA and Canada only. This offer expires 2/1/82. Please add applicable sales tax.

Thomas Sterling

☐ P 529 THE EVIL OF THE DAY $2.25

Julian Symons

☐ P 468 THE BELTING INHERITANCE $1.95
☐ P 469 BLAND BEGINNING $1.95
☐ P 481 BOGUE'S FORTUNE $1.95
☐ P 480 THE BROKEN PENNY $1.95
☐ P 461 THE COLOR OF MURDER $1.95
☐ P 460 THE 31ST OF FEBRUARY $1.95

Dorothy Stockbridge Tillet
(John Stephen Strange)

☐ P 536 THE MAN WHO KILLED FORTESCUE $2.25

Henry Kitchell Webster

☐ P 539 WHO IS THE NEXT? $2.25

Anna Mary Wells

☐ P 534 MURDERER'S CHOICE $2.25
☐ P 535 A TALENT FOR MURDER $2.25

Buy them at your local bookstore or use this coupon for ordering:

HARPER & ROW, Mail Order Dept. #PMS, 10 East 53rd St., New York, N.Y. 10022.
Please send me the books I have checked above. I am enclosing $ _____
which includes a postage and handling charge of $1.00 for the first book and
25¢ for each additional book. Send check or money order. No cash or
C.O.D.'s please.

Name _____

Address _____

City _____ State _____ Zip _____

Please allow 4 weeks for delivery. USA and Canada only. This offer expires
2/1/82. Please add applicable sales tax.